...ned below

CODENAME SEBASTIAN

CODENAME SEBASTIAN

Mo Kermode

VICTOR GOLLANCZ
LONDON

First published in Great Britain 1995
by Victor Gollancz
An imprint of the Cassell Group
Wellington House, 125 Strand, London WC2R 0BB

© Mo Kermode 1995

A catalogue record for this book is
available from the British Library.

ISBN 0 575 06074 3

Photoset in Great Britain by
Rowland Phototypesetting Ltd, Bury St Edmunds, Suffolk
Printed in Great Britain by
St Edmundsbury Press Ltd, Bury St Edmunds, Suffolk

For Louise, Helen and Matthew

Chapter One

"Sebastian—you sure you got it right?"

Little creases appeared on each side of Holly's nose. Frog-face, Joe thought. Why did she have to talk as if he was brain dead? He half-closed his eyes, imagining her green and even fatter, leaping across lily pads.

"You listening? Let's see the bit of paper."

She held out her hand and Joe fished in his pocket. Bossy, bossy, bossy.

"But Mum doesn't know anyone called Sebastian. You've spelt it wrong, anyway."

He shrugged.

"Probably just someone from work."

"We'd have heard of him."

"A new someone from work."

"She'd have said."

"A long-lost uncle . . . ?"

"Don't be stupid!"

Holly smoothed out the paper and read it again. "Sibastien rang," it said. "No messige."

"Sebastian." She chewed her lip. "Bit of a wimpish name if you ask me."

"What about Sebastian Coe?" Joe said. "He's not a wimp, he was an Olympic runner."

"And what'd Sebastian Coe be ringing Mum for? To

7

find out if she's entering the next London marathon?"

Joe had a vision of his round, definitely unathletic mother in vest and running shorts. He grinned.

"Tell me again exactly what he said."

Holly fixed her gimlet eye on him and Joe sighed heavily.

"I've already told you three times. He asked for Mum, and when I said she wasn't in he left the message."

Holly bit her nails.

"Except it's no message."

Over and over the same question kept gnawing at her mind. She had been seven when Dad left. Four years ago by her reckoning. He had married Karen straight after the divorce, and then last year the baby had arrived. He had a whole new family now. But neither she nor Joe had ever thought of their *mother* . . . Holly's stomach began churning uncomfortably.

"We'll ask her at teatime."

"She might not want to tell us." Joe looked doubtful.

"But if we ask her straight out she'll have to say something," Holly reasoned. "You can tell a lot from people's reactions. It's how they catch smugglers, seeing whether they sweat or blush or anything."

Joe screwed the paper into a ball.

"She working tonight?"

Holly shook her head.

"It's Friday."

"You ask."

It was funny how quickly you got used to things, Joe thought. When Mum first started working nights he had hated it. Getting himself up in the morning, creeping about whispering, burning the toast. Even with Mrs Bryant flapping her ears on the front-room sofa, it still felt as though they were

8

on their own. Mum had said they had to have a grownup in the house when she wasn't there at night, so she had asked Mrs Bryant, because Mrs Bryant had looked after Joe and Holly when they were little. But that was the trouble with people knowing you since you were a baby. They seemed to think you still were. The hot-water bottle she put in his bed was OK and so was having his bath run for him, but barging in to check he'd washed properly was definitely not OK.

Mum was on his side. She'd given the old bat a flea in her ear. Well, she'd said it was very kind of Mrs Bryant to take so much trouble, but now that he and Holly were growing up they had to start looking after themselves. So the tidemark round Joe's neck stayed comfortably in place, and in the mornings Mrs Bryant slept in—or pretended to—while they took charge. She poked her head round the door if she heard a crash, or if the smell of burning became too strong, but mostly she stuck to the bargain. It was only every third week, anyway. Nights paid more, Mum said whenever he complained, and the nursing agency always gave her three days off after a week of them. So it was worth it.

Holly had found it harder than Joe. She was older, she told him, so Mum had been there for more of her bedtimes. But now she'd got used to it, she quite enjoyed storing her news up for Friday teatime, then having her mother home all weekend. Dad was a different matter. It depressed her even to think about it. She'd tried to keep the Saturday afternoon visits going, especially once he and Karen moved back to West Merton, but these days there was always some excuse. He was busy, he was tired, they were going out, they were decorating, the baby was teething, the baby had a cold. The familiar pain started up inside Holly's chest each time she

9

thought about it. It wasn't fair. *They* had been Dad's children first. They should at least still be allowed to see him.

"Macaroni cheese tonight, kids. Cheap and cheerful." Teresa Burgess pulled the hot dish from the grill.

"End of the week," she explained.

Joe pulled down his eyes, pushed up his nose and made a sick face. His mother spoke without turning round.

"That's quite enough from you, my lad. When you've made your first million you can keep me in comfort and have steak every day. Till then you'll eat what's put in front of you!"

Eyes in her bum, Joe thought aggrieved. And rotten fruit salad for afters. He had been hoping for chocolate sponge pudding. Teresa settled herself at the table and began serving out.

"Right then, what's been going on in the land of the living this week?"

He brightened.

"We won against Grantley Street two–nil," he said. "You should have heard Wilkie cheer when Spud put the second goal in! We're through to the semi-final now."

"Wilkie said we can start bringing stuff in for the summer jumble, too," Holly said. "Have you got anything, Mum?"

"Save some for me!"

Joe's eyes bulged as the hot macaroni cheese scorched his mouth. There were only two aims in his life. Number one was to see Priory Road Juniors win the Cup. Number two was to impress Wilkie. There wasn't another coach to touch him, everyone said so. He could have gone professional if he'd wanted. Imagine becoming a boring headmaster when you could have played for Man United or Spurs! Priory Road had been bottom of the heap before Wilkie took them over, they'd never even got through round one. But this year, for the first time ever, they stood a real chance of winning the Cup. The bad news was it could be the *last* time ever, too. Wilkie was moving to a new school next term.

"Jumble?" Teresa said. "There's a pile of smelly football strip behind the kitchen door—think your Mr Wilkinson might be interested?"

Joe's face turned a dangerous shade of purple.

"No, really, Mum," Holly said. "It's a competition. We're seeing which class brings in the most. Wilkie wants mums and dads to help on the day, too—you did last time," she wheedled.

"Can't if I'm on nights," her mother said. "But I expect I can sort you out a few bits and pieces. How's the macaroni cheese?"

Joe did a milder version of his sick face and Holly kicked him.

"It's fine," she said. "Better than the gunge they serve up at school."

Teresa looked pleased. Strike while the iron's hot, Holly thought. Her class had been doing proverbs.

"Mum," she said. "Who's Sebastian?"

Was it her imagination or had there been the slightest tremor in Teresa's hand, the faintest flush of colour in her cheeks? Holly watched, hawk-like.

"He rang," she added.

"Was there a message?"

"No message," Joe said.

Teresa coughed.

"It's probably—one of the new nurses."

They waited.

"I expect—I expect he wanted to change shifts."

"Is it a boyfriend?" Holly said.

A dollop of macaroni cheese slid slowly from her mother's fork and plopped gently on to her plate.

"Would that be so terrible?" she said at last. "It gets a bit lonely spending evenings and weekends on your own, you know."

"But we're here, Mum!" Joe's eyes became very large. "We keep you company, don't we?"

"Yes," Teresa said, "you do. Except the three nights a week you're out doing something, plus Saturday mornings and most of Sunday."

Joe looked guilty and she put an arm round him.

"I'm not getting at you," she said. "I don't want either of you giving up swimming or band or anything else for me. But there's a world going on out there. I'd like to see a bit of it again."

"You could go to night school, Mum," Holly suggested. "Deb's mum goes to pottery Tuesday nights. You could go with her."

"Maybe, if I didn't have ten thumbs," her mother said. "But I don't want to make pots, I want to make friends. I want people to talk to. It's company I'm missing."

She means *men's* company, Holly thought ominously. The question mark in her mind glowed a fierce fluorescent red.

"Are you going to get—married again?"

She forced the words out and Teresa laughed.

"Not this week," she said. "But you may as well know. I've—I've joined a club."

The children exchanged glances.

"What kind of club?" Joe asked. This time Teresa definitely did blush.

12

"It's for people on their own," she said. "So they can, er, meet other people on their own."

"What do you do there?" Holly thought of the Thursday night youth club. "Listen to music, play table tennis?"

"It's not quite that sort of club," her mother said. "This one's all done by post. You get sent a list of members, then you phone or write letters to the ones you like the sound of."

"You mean penfriends?" Joe watched her hopefully. "Like when Holly got a Christmas card from that girl in Germany?"

His mother shifted slightly.

"You, er, only write or phone at the beginning," she said. "After that the idea is to actually meet the other person and, well, see how you get on."

They gawped.

"*A blind date?*"

Holly suddenly remembered a whole series of rushed teas, new clothes and "meetings" Teresa had dashed off to.

"Sebastian," she said. "He's one, isn't he?"

A scarlet flush rose from her mother's neck like a rash. She began scraping the plates hard.

"What's he like, Mum? Tell us what he's like!"

"Is he nice? Is he rich?"

"Have you met any others?"

Teresa wasn't giving any more away.

"He's all right," she said, her eyes firmly on the bowl of fruit salad. "And before you ask—no, I don't know if I'm seeing him again and, yes, I have met one or two others. End of interrogation."

Joe helped himself then spat out a cherry stone.

"Where do you meet them, Mum? Do you go to the Black Dog?" He had seen some pretty unlikely characters passing

13

through those doors. But Teresa tapped a finger against her nose.

"Never you mind, young man, I've already said more than I should—and don't either of you dare breathe a word about this at school. Once that Josie Roper's mum gets her teeth into a juicy bit of gossip you might as well put up a poster." She finished her meal and pushed the plate away.

"Who's on washing up?"

For once there were no arguments. Joe brought the dishes through and kicked the kitchen door shut behind him. Two deep creases had appeared in his forehead.

"Is she going to get married again?"

Holly watched the foam rise slowly over her wrists.

"If she is," she said slowly, "then we'd get a *stepfather*." She let the word sink in. "And you know what that would mean. Some bossy creep moving in, some bigheaded twit pushing us around!"

Joe shuddered.

"How can we stop her?"

"First thing's to know what we're up against. We've got to find a way of checking out this Sebastian—and any other Sebastians who might be hanging round."

Joe's eyebrows lifted.

"Just like that? We don't even know who they are."

He fished out the last piece of pineapple and wiped his finger round the custard jug. Holly watched him absently.

"If we found out where she meets them," she said, "we could go and spy. Then we'd know who they were."

Joe paused, his finger in mid-flight.

"But she could meet them anywhere—and suppose she saw us?"

"She wouldn't," Holly said. "Not if we did it properly. But

14

we'd see *them*, the Sebastians. Then we could work out how to get rid of them."

Joe thought about it.

"They probably go to the pub," he said. "But we're not allowed in there."

Holly's eyes narrowed into slits like a cat. She blew gently across the top of the milk bottle.

"We might not need to go *in* . . ." She smiled slyly. "Leave it to me. I've got an idea."

Chapter Two

"She'll kill us!" Joe whispered.

"She won't know, will she?" Holly whispered back. "We've got to find out about them somehow."

They could hear the shower through the wall. It was Wednesday. Sebastian hadn't rung again. Joe wandered across the room and began nervously flicking the light switch.

"But if we're not allowed in pubs how can we find out about them? Anyway, we don't even know which one she's going to." Holly waved a sheet of paper at him.

"What's that?"

"First ten pubs in *Yellow Pages*. Your sister's not just a pretty face, you know. I found out how to get to them, it's on the back. They're all quite near, but the point is some of them are bound to have beer gardens."

"Beer gardens?" Joe looked blank. "So?"

"So it doesn't get dark until after eight o'clock. So if they do go to a pub they might sit outside. So if we can find the right one we'll be able to see him—Sebastian!"

"But it'll take weeks to get round that lot," Joe complained. "And even then we might not find them. I'm not wasting about a year's playing-out time sussing out all the pubs in Wallcot—I might turn into an alky!"

Holly sighed.

"Who got a mountain bike for Christmas? Who says he's in line for the world land speed record?"

The penny dropped.

"You mean I've got to spend all night on a bike crawl, looking for Mum and some bloke? I'm supposed to be in bed by nine o'clock!"

"Not just you," Holly pacified him. "And we won't be out that long, it'll be dark. Anyway, I want to watch something on telly at eight-thirty."

"Mum doesn't like you watching that programme," he said self-righteously. Holly shrugged.

"She won't know, will she, unless *someone* tells her."

Joe still looked put out.

"Listen," his sister said sharply. "Do you want some drivelling old fogy landed on you? Some half-wit you've never seen before who says, right kids, no more staying up late at weekends, no more getting round your mum. I'm your new dad. You do as *I* say now?"

Joe paled.

"How about if we do five pubs each?"

Holly tore the paper in two.

"That's more like it."

They stood in the front porch beside their bikes. Teresa had been gone twenty minutes.

"It's a bit like being detectives, isn't it?" Joe said. "We ought to give it a name like the police do. Operation Beer Garden or something."

"You watch too much telly." Holly was scornful.

"Look who's talking! I'm not the one who wants to be back for some stupid programme."

"Not half so stupid as some of the stuff you watch!"

17

She disentangled her front wheel from his, then stood thinking.

"It's not such a bad idea, giving it a name," she said grudgingly. "It'd mean we could talk about it without anyone knowing what we were on about. How about . . . Operation TSB?"

"Sounds like a bank raid," Joe said. "What's it stand for?"

"Teresa's Secret Boyfriends."

He groaned.

"Can't you do better than that?"

"All right, Mastermind, you try!"

"I've already told you my idea. Operation Beer Garden."

"But the pub they go to might not have a beer garden," Holly pointed out. "Come to that, they might not even go to a pub. If they take themselves off to the pictures or somewhere, we're up the creek."

"Well, what then?"

Holly thought. They needed a name that showed the life and death necessity of the investigation. The fact that their entire future now hung on some unknown faceless man.

"What about . . . Codename Sebastian?"

Joe grinned.

"Synchronize watches. Six forty-three and fourteen seconds. Meet you outside the park at quarter to eight."

"Roger."

She cycled off in the direction of the Black Dog. It was the nearest pub to home, but she didn't think for a minute Teresa would be there. Especially not with Josie Roper's mum behind the bar. They had to do the job properly, though. A shiver ran through her as she imagined what might happen if Teresa found out, but she shrugged it aside. It was all very well Mum keeping her goings-on a big secret but it was their

18

future too. How would she like it if some man bulldozed his way into *her* life? Children had no rights, she told herself. First their real dad had gone off and left them, and now, whether they liked it or not, they were going to get some second-hand version dumped on them instead. She turned left at the corner of Exeter Gardens and puffed up the hill to the crossroads.

Ten to seven must be early for pubs. There were only two cars in the Black Dog car-park. Peering through the hedge into the beer garden, Holly saw it was empty apart from Josie Roper's mum setting out beer mats and picking up litter. Mrs Roper's hair was piled stiffly on top of her head, and she was wearing high heels and a dress with a very low front that Holly could see right down when she leant over. She seemed to be taking a long time for such a small task, and kept glancing towards the bar door as if she was expecting someone. After a while the landlord came out and Holly recognized him, too. It was Kevin Foggarty's dad.

Kevin Foggarty was a pain. Even more of a pain than Josie Roper. He was in year six at Priory Road with Holly, and was always boasting about what he'd got or was going to get, and how his dad let him drink beer and lager. She should have guessed he lived in a pub. Every playtime he'd swagger round like cock of the school, bullying and tormenting younger children. Some of them tried to join his gang for protection, but it didn't do them much good. Mr Foggarty had the same swagger as his son, Holly noted, except that the enormous stomach hanging over his belt had turned it into more of a roll.

As soon as she spotted him, Mrs Roper moved into the shady part of the garden nearest the hedge, and after a quick glance round Mr Foggarty came across to join her. Holly

19

expected him to say something about customers waiting in the bar or there being no more peanuts. But to her surprise he sidled up to Mrs Roper, put his arm round her waist and whispered something in her ear. Mrs Roper fluttered her false eyelashes and giggled, and his hand gradually slipped down to her bottom. It was quite a large bottom, and Mr Foggarty's pudgy hand began squeezing and kneading it as though he were making bread or shaping clay. Then as Holly watched, fascinated, his other hand began creeping slowly up the front of Mrs Roper's dress.

Holly couldn't believe it. She levered herself up, craning forward to get a better look—and realized too late she was overbalancing. With a crash the bike slid from under her and she lurched forward into the hedge. Mrs Roper jumped away with a little squeal as Holly's surprised face appeared six centimetres from her bosom.

"What the dickens . . . ! Holly Burgess, whatever are you up to?" she shrieked. "Spying on people like that, frightening the customers!"

Holly didn't think it was the moment to point out there *were* no customers. And she didn't like the look on Mr Foggarty's face, either.

Dragging herself painfully out of the hedge, she pointed dramatically to the cherry tree in the corner of the beer garden.

"A—a greenfinch!" she exclaimed. "There—look!"

"I can't see no greenfinch," Mrs Roper said suspiciously. "And since when have you been so interested in birds?"

"Oh, er, me and Joe go birdwatching in the park," Holly said, thinking fast. "I'm on my way there now. Do you want to know what we've spotted so far?"

She fumbled in her pocket for the list of pubs, praying

neither of them would turn out to be an expert ornithologist. But Mrs Roper moved away in annoyance.

"No, I would not," she said. "I'm surprised your mother lets you go to that park at night. Full of undesirables, it is. But I suppose she's out gallivanting again."

Holly looked Mrs Roper up and down and the woman reddened. Then, patting her hair and tugging at her dress, she teetered off into the bar. Mr Foggarty smiled an artificial smile.

"Nice hobby, birdwatching," he said. "Always been fond of the birds meself."

He laughed loudly so that his stomach wobbled, then followed Mrs Roper inside.

Holly leant shakily against her bike. That had been close. But who would have thought it? Josie Roper's mum and Kevin Foggarty's dad! She waited until her legs steadied then rode along the pavement for a while, thinking. She remembered Kevin Foggarty's mousy little mother coming to sports days and concerts, Josie Roper's greying dad . . . Grownups were never satisfied, she decided. But people were always up to that kind of thing on telly, so why did it seem so shocking in real life? Perhaps everyone did it.

A pang shot through Holly as she imagined Teresa with her boyfriends, though at least *she* wasn't deceiving anyone. But Dad must have been, she realized for the first time. He had still been married to Mum when he first met Karen. He could hardly have sat down to tea then announced he was going out to see his girlfriend. He must have met her secretly behind their backs, like Mr Foggarty with Mrs Roper. Kissed her and cuddled her, then came back home as though nothing had happened. A bad taste rose in Holly's mouth and she pedalled hard along to the Butcher's Arms.

*

21

Joe circled the Dusty Miller twice before he dared peer through the screen of privet round its neat little garden. But when he did he saw two women talking, an old man sitting alone and some sparrows hopping about on a table. No one else. Half-relieved, half-disappointed, he consulted his list. Next was the Eagle. Past the chocolate factory, first right, second on the left. He followed Holly's instructions exactly, but pulled up short when he saw the Eagle's "garden". It was just a cluster of tables on the pavement. She might have warned him! If Teresa had been sitting there he wouldn't have stood a chance. He rode round the side and heard music coming from a room at the back. But the high windows were made of stained glass, and although he tried jumping up and down he couldn't see through them. He got his breath back and looked at his watch. Seven eighteen and six seconds. Time for one more.

But the Elephant and Castle was more of a hotel than a pub. There was a huge car-park already about a third full, a terrace, two restaurants and several bars. How was he supposed to suss that lot out? Trying to appear casual he worked his way round to the terrace, then pressed his face against the wooden trellis and did a quick survey. The back of a bald man's head, a fat woman in a purple dress, a girl with an ice-cream cone. The girl gave him an idea. Fastening his bike to the trellis he slipped through the open door of the hotel and looked about him.

"What's the trouble, sonny?" a waiter asked. Joe thought the man must have heard his heart banging inside him.

"Um, can you tell me where the toilet is, please?"

"Past the steak restaurant, turn left at the bottom of the stairs and it's on your right," the man said, then flashed past him with a tray of drinks.

Joe couldn't believe his luck. The waiter had taken it for granted he was with one of the families outside. He walked noiselessly down the corridor, his feet sinking into the thick carpet, and came to the steak restaurant. He scanned the room quickly as he went past, turned left at the foot of the stairs and pushed open the door of the toilet. He hadn't seen anyone who looked like Teresa. He got himself a drink of water, squirted some fancy-smelling soap on his hands and dried them under the electric drier. Seven thirty-one, better get a move on. Shame there was nothing to report. He got out the key to his bike lock, walked briskly back the way he had come and slipped out on to the terrace. Round the trellis, behind the bald man and the girl, squeeze past the purple dress. He stopped dead. His bike had gone.

Chapter Three

Joe stared at the space where his bike had been, half-expecting it to materialize from thin air. But there was no doubt about it. It had gone. He looked quickly round the car-park then ran to the road and scanned the passing traffic, the key still clutched uselessly in his hand. But whoever had taken it had made a fast getaway—and left him in a spot. If he told the police, they would want to know what he had been doing in the Elephant and Castle car-park. But if he didn't tell them, Teresa would want to know why not.

He swallowed the panic rising in his throat. Seven thirty-six and nineteen seconds. Holly would be waiting for him at the park. She might even have seen Sebastian. But the threat of an unknown stepfather paled beside this greater catastrophe. Tears rose in Joe's eyes at the thought of his precious mountain bike. He had pestered Teresa so hard she had saved for months to buy it, and now he had lost it, spying on her. He set off running towards the park.

"Where've you been?" Holly demanded. "It's nearly five to eight. Where's your bike?"

Holding his side, Joe explained what had happened. Holly saw the problem at once. She had had no more success at private investigation than he had and they sat glumly on the park wall, wondering what to do next.

"You could say you thought it would be safer in the car-park."

Joe shook his head.

"Where was I supposed to be playing?"

She saw his point. The Elephant and Castle was nowhere near any of their usual haunts, and it was miles away from the park.

She got up and wheeled her own bike to the top of a grassy bump. Below was what people still called the lake, though nowadays it was more of a stagnant pond. Some boys were playing about round the edge, trying to push a smaller one in by the look of it. Holly watched, feeling sorry for the smaller boy. It wasn't dangerous, the water was only about two feet deep, but he was yelling and crying and obviously frightened. Joe came up beside her and watched too. Then he stiffened. One of the boys was Kevin Foggarty, he was sure of it.

Like Holly, Joe avoided Kevin Foggarty, but he knew more about him than his sister did. Kevin was big, even for year six, and liked to throw his weight about. Outside school he went round with a crowd of older boys. Some of them had been in trouble with the police—Joe had heard Kevin boasting about it. Sometimes he brought cigarettes and money into school he said they got from cars.

"Asking for it, they are," Kevin would say scornfully. "Half of 'em don't even lock their cars. What do they expect?"

Joe watched him now, taunting the boy by the water's edge. He wouldn't want to tangle with Kevin Foggarty.

Holly began pushing her bike down the slope towards the lake but Joe lagged behind, reluctant to come face to face with Kevin's gang. He had never been bothered at school, but out here it was different. Kevin would be looking for ways of showing off in front of his heroes and if Joe Burgess provided the opportunity, he knew Kevin would take it.

"I don't want to go down there," he said. "Let's have a go on the swings."

But Holly was peering at the commotion by the lake. She had recognized Kevin Foggarty, too, but she thought she had also recognized something else.

"Look down there," she commanded. "By that tree."

Joe looked where she was pointing. A heap of bikes lay on the grass, clearly the Foggarty gang's transport. But from where they were standing one of them looked suspiciously like Joe's.

"What would they want my bike for? It's too small for any of them."

But as he peered at the tangle of wheels and handlebars he caught his breath sharply.

"Holly! There's six bikes there, but there's only *five* of them!"

He suddenly remembered Kevin hinting at other things they took from cars and car-parks, more valuable things that they sold . . . He went a little way ahead, screwing up his eyes, trying to spot the blue tape Teresa had stuck round his crossbar. But the setting sun shone in his eyes and he couldn't make it out. Recklessly he ran down the hill and dragged the black bike out from among the others. And, wonder of wonders, it was there. The blue tape was there! And there were his initials scratched under the handlebars: JDB.

"It's here!" he yelled. "Holly, it's here! It's my bike!"

He turned to find a large denim-jacketed boy with the beginnings of a moustache looking menacingly down at him.

"I think you've made a mistake, my son," the boy said

smoothly. "This bike belongs to my little brother. Get over here, Kev. Tell the gentleman whose bike it is."

Kevin Foggarty left the smaller boy and came across, grinning. The gang gathered in a circle round Joe. Kevin wasn't anyone's little brother, Joe knew that. It was all part of the show. He watched warily as Kevin sauntered cockily towards him, hands in pockets. Kevin's eyes travelled over the bike.

"'Sright," he said. "Me dad got it me for Christmas, but I've grown a bit since then. So hands off my property, Burgess!"

He kicked the bike from Joe's grasp.

"You liar, Kevin Foggarty!" Joe went rigid with rage. "It's my bike, you know it is! You've just pinched it from outside the Elephant and Castle and I'm having it back!"

He lifted the bike upright, then dropped it with a yell as Kevin twisted his arm painfully up his back.

"No one calls me a liar, ratface," he hissed. "Now say sorry like a good boy."

"Liar! Thief!"

Joe kicked out furiously. Tears sprang to his eyes as Kevin forced his arm higher. Through a red haze he saw Holly appear in front of him.

"Let him go!"

"Get lost, frogface," Kevin sneered. "It's nothing to do with you!"

"Let him go," Holly said again. She could hear her heart banging inside her ribs. "Or—or I'll get someone." She looked helplessly round. Two old ladies with dogs. A couple wrapped up in each other on the grass.

"Hear that, fellers?" Kevin mocked. "Holly Burgess is going to get someone. Watch out for flying zimmers!"

The other boys closed in laughing, leering down at her.

She looked anxiously at Joe. He was sobbing openly now.

"I'll tell your dad," she threatened. "I know where you live."

Kevin spat on the grass.

"Me dad wouldn't do nothing. I do what I like!"

To Joe's alarm Holly began to walk away.

"Yeah, shove off!" Kevin called after her.

"Going to tell your mum?" someone else jeered.

"No." She turned and looked straight at Kevin. "I'm going to tell Josie Roper's dad. I bet he'd be interested in what you get up to at nights. Though he'd probably be more interested in what your *dad* gets up to, wouldn't he, Kevin . . . ?"

Kevin's face turned a strange grey.

"What you talking about? You don't know nothing about my dad!"

"I know he likes Mrs Roper for a start," Holly said. "Always squeezing and stroking her, I've seen him at it. He wouldn't want Mr Roper to find that out, would he?"

A strangled sound came from Kevin's throat and he dropped Joe's arm.

"You don't know that!" he spat.

"I wish I didn't," Holly said.

"Take no notice, son!"

A tall boy in a skull and crossbones sweatshirt ruffled his hair. "So your dad's got a fancy bit. Good luck to him!"

The rest of them laughed and punched each other, but Kevin Foggarty looked disturbed. He knew, and Holly and Joe knew, that Josie Roper's dad wasn't a man to mess with. He was much older than Josie's mum, but when he was younger he had worked as a porter at the meat market. He still wore T-shirts that showed off his muscles, and walked a huge dog on a metal chain. They all knew he would think nothing of knocking down the roly-poly barrel of lard Mr Foggarty had become.

Kevin threw Joe's bike to the ground.

"Wouldn't have got much for it, anyway. Tatty old thing!"

"It is no—!" Joe began indignantly, then closed his mouth as Holly shot him a warning look. His arm still felt as though it was on fire.

"Sure, Kev? You can have it if you want," Denim Jacket said.

But Kevin shook his head. He kicked the bike viciously and stalked back towards the lake. The other boys knocked it around for a few more minutes then they, too, lost interest and sauntered off.

"Let's go," Holly hissed. "Before they change their minds."

Joe picked up his bike and they hurried towards the bowling green. There were usually more people there. He sat down on a bench, his legs still shaky.

"What did you mean about Kevin Foggarty's dad?" he said. "Did you really see him groping Mrs Roper?"

Holly hesitated.

"It was just a guess," she said. "I've seen him eyeing her up."

"Well, your guess just saved my life—and my bike.' Joe looked at her with grudging admiration. "Although it was your stupid idea to go playing detectives in the first place!"

"Not so stupid," Holly said. "How else are we going to find out what Mum's up to?"

They both remembered what they had come out for. Joe told Holly about the Dusty Miller, and the problems of the Eagle and the Elephant and Castle. She told him *some* of what she had seen at the Black Dog, and how the Butcher's Arms beer garden was at the back, and the Clarence didn't have one at all. They sat on the bench in the shelter considering their next move.

"There's still some pubs left," Holly said. "We ought to try them all."

"Well, I'm walking next time," Joe told her. "Even if it takes all night!" He looked at his watch. He had no idea how long the trouble with the gang had taken. "Eight eighteen and twelve seconds. Better get moving."

He examined his bike. Apart from a few dents and scratches it seemed to be in working order.

"Let's go back along the canal," Holly suggested. "There's still time, and we might see some painted boats."

They pushed their bikes to the park gates and freewheeled down the hill.

Holly had always liked the canal. When she and Joe were small they had spent their holidays chugging through the still water on a slow barge. Minding bridges, watching the locks carry them up and down. Joe said he couldn't remember any of it, but Holly could still picture every minute of those holidays. Sleeping in a little cabin, cooking supper in the galley, helping Dad steer. He'd been on the canal again last year, but that was with Karen. And the baby.

They squeezed through the swing gate and began pedalling along the towpath. A few couples strolled past in the gathering dusk. A man walking his dog, two boys throwing sticks—Holly slammed her brakes on so hard she almost skidded into the water.

"Get down," she hissed. "Quick, get down!"

Leaping off her bike, she dragged it into the tangled undergrowth. Joe followed, mystified.

"What's going on? What d'you do that for?" He peered out through a screen of prickly bushes.

Her heart pounding, Holly pointed.

Chapter Four

He was a short, angry-looking man. Red face, nose going on purple, slicked-back hair and a ferocious brush of a moustache. He wore a blue blazer with silver buttons and very shiny shoes. As he crunched along the towpath, arms swinging smartly at his sides, he flashed large white teeth and barked out a stream of words like machine-gun fire. Beside him Teresa picked her way over the gravel, smiling nervously. Holly dug her brother hard in the ribs.

"Sebastian!" she hissed.

But Joe shook his head. It wasn't the voice he had heard on the phone. This one was older, bossier. Used to getting its own way. The man took Teresa's hand and trapped it firmly in his arm, talking too loudly, walking too close. Joe's knuckles clenched white on the handlebars.

"Slimy toad!' he whispered. "Ancient relic! He wears false teeth, you can tell. I bet he takes them out at night like Mrs Bryant."

He turned to Holly and rolled his eyes gruesomely, sucking his lips in over his teeth.

"Oh, by darling, will you barry me?"

Holly giggled, but for one awful moment she saw the man lying to attention in the front bedroom at twenty-eight Exeter Gardens. He'd wear pyjamas with immaculate creases, order breakfast at six-thirty on the dot. Interrogate them after school. Send them on forced marches. Punish them if they couldn't keep up ... A film of sweat broke out on her forehead.

"This one," she said firmly, "would be a Major Disaster!"

Huddled in the undergrowth, they watched until Teresa and the man were out of sight, then dragged their bikes up to the road. Joe tried to unscramble his thoughts. It was all very well treating these boyfriends as a kind of game, but actually seeing one of them, and Teresa with him, had made them horribly, frighteningly real. Holly had been right, they had to check them out. Imagine getting landed with *that* one.

But apart from the man's sheer awfulness, what frightened Joe most was how much of a stranger he was. He was so alien he could have come from Mars. But then, *all* the Sebastians would be strangers. And if Teresa married one it would be like living with a mystery parcel, never knowing what was under the next layer. Joe didn't want some toothless, purple-nosed bully pushing him around, telling him what to do. Muscling in on his comfortable, cluttered life. What he did want, he realized, was Dad.

As soon as they were home he slipped upstairs to Teresa's room. The phone was by the bed. He picked it up and dialled, and within seconds—why had he never thought of it as a miracle before?—there was his father on the other end, so close Joe felt he could put out a hand and touch him. For a moment he closed his eyes, listening to the familiar voice and husky breathing, picturing every line of the face they belonged to.

"West Merton 302," his father said again, more sharply. "Who's there?"

"Hi, Dad. It's me, Joe."

33

A silence.

"Shouldn't you be in bed? Does your mother know you're phoning?"

"She's gone out." Joe paused. "I just wanted to say hallo."

He felt suddenly shy. His father laughed shortly.

"Not the best time for a chat, son. Little 'un's playing up. It's his teeth."

He sounded harassed. Joe could hear the baby wailing in the background, then Karen asking who was on the phone.

"Another time, eh?" his father said. Then, more kindly, "Look after yourself, Joe."

The phone went dead. For a while Joe watched it purring quietly in his hand. Then he went back to his own room, crawled into bed and pulled the covers over his head.

"What's up?" Teresa asked over breakfast, seeing Joe's face.

"Someone pinched his bike from—from the park railings," Holly said. "We got it back," she added quickly. "But it's a bit bent and they cut through the cable lock."

"You were lucky," his mother told him. "A dozen bikes a day go missing in this town." She pushed back her chair. "Bring you back another lock tonight, OK? Done your spellings, got your games kit?"

Joe nodded. She blew them a kiss then breezed out of the door. There were twenty minutes before school.

"Right," Holly pulled a notebook from her bag. "The next thing is we've got to grade them."

"Grade what?" Joe looked puzzled.

"Not what, *who*. The Sebastians, of course. Mum's boy-friends."

"What do you mean, grade them?"

34

"Put them in order. Give them points so we can see which one we like best."

"I'm not going to like any of them." Joe scowled.

"You've only seen one," Holly pointed out. "The others might be better. Mum's not stupid, you know. I bet she wouldn't have gone out with that one if she'd seen him first."

Hope passed fleetingly across her brother's face. "Look." She opened the notebook. "I did it last night."

At the top of the first page she had written in capital letters

CODENAME SEBASTIAN

Underneath were six columns. Joe read along the headings.

NAME. DATE. PLACE. DESCRIPTION. VERDICT.

The last column was headed FATHER FACTOR. There were two names down the side: Sebastian and Major Disaster.

"What's Father Factor?" Joe said. He noticed there was a nought against it for Major Disaster.

"It's how we rate them as dads," Holly told him. "How kind of dad-like they are. It goes from one to ten."

He looked at what else she had written. Against Sebastian she had put:

DATE: 18 April (5.30 p.m.)
PLACE: telephone
DESCRIPTION: deep voice

But the last two columns were blank.

Major Disaster was more fully recorded. His details read:

DATE: 23 April (8.26 p.m.)
PLACE: canal toepath
DESCRIPTION: old, bossy, greasy hair, folse teeth.
VERDICT: no way
FATHER FACTOR: 0

Joe smiled for the first time that day.

"I thought of something else," Holly said. "I don't know why we didn't think of it before."

Joe looked up from the dossier.

"The Rose and Crown, that pub down by the canal. We used to go there with Mum and Dad when we'd been on the boats, don't you remember?"

Now that she mentioned it, he did.

"Do you think that's where she takes them?"

Holly's forehead puckered.

"Could be. Perhaps she wants to kind of measure them against Dad."

Joe thought he saw what she meant.

"I phoned him last night," he confessed, and Holly looked at him sharply.

"You didn't tell him anything?"

"Course not!" Joe was scornful. "I just wanted to talk to him."

Holly sympathized. After Major Disaster she had felt the same way herself. She waited for him to say something about going over to the flat, but when he stayed silent she guessed what had happened. Same old story. They might just as well not have a dad at all. For the first time it crossed her mind that a stepfather might not be an entirely bad thing. Depending on who it was, of course. She nudged her brother.

"Coming to call for Debs with me? She's got a new rabbit."

They cleared the table and set off for school.

"This is going to be the biggest, the best, the *jumbliest* jumble sale Priory Road has ever seen!"

Wilkie was in full flight. Two hundred and fifty children sat, enjoying the spectacle.

"We're going to have clothes stalls, toy stalls, white elephant stalls, book stalls. Even a cake stall!"

"Sir!" A girl at the front put up her hand. "Sir, cakes aren't jumble, sir!"

Mr Wilkinson paused dramatically, a fist clenched to his forehead.

"Alas, Michaela," he said, "the only word that could possibly describe the cakes I make is indeed jumble!"

Everyone laughed. It was a shame he was going, Holly thought, but she'd be at a new school herself next term, so she wouldn't notice the difference. Joe would miss him, though. He'd gone to football practice every week for ages now. Holly had heard all about the team treats after matches. She hoped the head at Wallcot High would be as good as Wilkie.

At playtime Kevin Foggarty passed her but he didn't say anything. She heard him pouring scorn on the jumble sale.

"Second-hand junk! If I want something I go out and get it new."

"But it's for the school," someone else said. "For more computers."

"Computers," Kevin sneered. "I got me own computer at home. Who needs Priory Road rubbish?"

He swaggered off, hands in pockets. The group of children looked after him.

"Jumped up squirt!"

Josie Roper stuck her tongue out so far Holly wondered how much she knew. To her surprise she found herself feeling almost sorry for the girl.

"My dad says he's a hard case," someone else said. "He'll be in trouble before long."

Watching Kevin Foggarty kick someone's football over the railings, then scatter a game of marbles, Holly hoped she wouldn't be around to see it.

And after dinner, thankfully, she was spared his company.

"I need four *incredibly* strong, *massively* intelligent human beings," Wilkie announced, sticking his head round their classroom door. "There's about half a ton of jumble to be sorted," he explained apologetically, and most of the hands went down.

But Holly and three others volunteered to spend the afternoon moving and stacking the mountain of clothes and bric-à-brac that had grown in the hall.

Why had she opened her big mouth, she wondered two hours later, still lugging jigsaws and table lamps and fur coats through to the old garages. She was sticky and sweaty and itched all over. It was one thing getting the afternoon off lessons, but colouring in the Grampians like everyone else might have been a whole lot easier than developing bodybuilder's biceps. She dumped the fur coats in one of the tea chests along the wall and scribbled "Ladies clothes" on it in large chalk letters. Then she examined herself for flea bites.

There were definitely perks attached to being in the top class, Joe decided, watching his sister carry bags and boxes across the playground. He envied her freedom. Perhaps when he was in year six he'd be doing jobs and sorting out jumble for Wilkie instead of being stuck in boring old maths. But then he remembered Wilkie would be leaving at the end of term. Who would they give his job to? Not Mrs Carmichael, he prayed, please not Mrs Carmichael . . . Her foxy face loomed a row closer, and Joe tried to imagine her making a fool of herself the way Wilkie did. He had to clamp his lips shut tight at the thought.

How was it some people grew up kind and friendly but others turned into miserable old fossils? He would never become mean and grouchy, he promised himself. He would always be nice to children. And if he had any of his own he would never, *ever* forget about them . . .

"Finished already, Joseph Burgess?"

Mrs Carmichael's X-ray eyes bored into him and Joe reddened. He tried to work up an interest in 198 divided by 11. Hadn't someone already abolished slavery?

Chapter Five

As soon as the phone rang, Holly pressed her ear hard against her bedroom wall. Teresa sounded fluttery, taken by surprise.

"Tonight?" she heard. Then a pause. ". . . to seven?" Pause. "OK . . . Canal Street. Yes . . . bottom."

It had to be the Rose and Crown! Holly knew every pub in *Yellow Pages* by heart now and there wasn't another one on Canal Street. She pulled open her dressing-table drawer and checked the Surveillance Kit she and Joe had put together. Binoculars, notebook, pencil, camera, biscuits. They were going to do a proper job this time. She repacked the rucksack and buried it under a pile of pyjamas, then went down to look for her brother.

Football practice had been cut short. Wilkie had been so tied up with the jumble sale he had only been able to spare them half an hour, and Joe wandered home marking time. They stood a good chance against St Margaret's in the semi-final, he reckoned. The Maggies had only got through in the first place because that dozy Tony Birchall on the Hamilton Road side put in an own goal. In any case, Priory Road had a secret weapon. Spud'd see them right. Nineteen goals she'd scored so far this season. Was that a record? She might get the League Footballer of the Year award, though most of the teams they played laughed when anyone suggested that. Merton County said there was no way they'd even let a girl on their team in the first place. Wilkie was always having to step in and stop rows. At least the rest of Priory Road saw she had been a good idea. He turned into Exeter Gardens and realized his stomach indicator was at starvation level. Tuesday, he thought. Sausages. Good.

Holly grabbed him as he came through the gate.

"Quick, get changed," she commanded. "We're on!"

Joe gazed at her blankly, his mind a mixture of football and food.

"Codename Sebastian. Mum's meeting another one tonight."

It registered.

"How do you know?"

"Heard her on the phone—and it *is* the Rose and Crown. I knew it was! Conference in my room six fifteen."

She swept past him. Joe dumped his bag behind the kitchen door and trudged upstairs. His insides had become strangely mixed up together. One half of him wanted desperately to find out about these boyfriends of his mother's but the other half wanted to forget the whole business, to pretend none of it existed. He pushed open his bedroom door and flopped on to the bed.

Teresa was very bright over tea.

"How's the jumble going?" she asked. "I met Mrs Bryant in the post office this morning, and she made it sound like the *Sale of the Century*!"

"It's going to be great, Mum," Holly said. "We're in charge, Debs and me and Ian McEnnis and Barry Collins. We've got it all sorted into different kinds of jumble, and tomorrow we're going to start pricing it. Everyone's got to check with us how much to charge."

"But *we* didn't get our proper football practice because of it," Joe complained. "And it's the Cup semi-final next week."

"Don't worry," Teresa told him. "With Spud Clarke and Joe Burgess on the same team, St Margaret's won't know what's hit them!"

"Will you come and cheer us on, Mum?" Joe said.

Teresa hesitated.

"It depends on work," she said vaguely. "I think I'm on lates next Wednesday."

Joe looked disappointed and Holly frowned. If her mother was meeting Sebastians, there was nothing to stop her doing it during the day, she realized. Plenty of men worked shifts, too. But if that was what she was up to, it would put the lid on their detective work. There was no way they could follow her in the daytime. Pondering, she smothered a sausage in tomato ketchup.

When Joe came into her room at quarter-past six she kept her thoughts to herself. Teresa really did work odd hours sometimes. No point in worrying over nothing.

"What time's she going out?" Joe poked among the debris on Holly's dressing table.

"Quarter to sevenish, I expect. Something to seven, anyway. I heard her say. We'd better get there about the same time and find a good look-out spot."

Her brother tried an earring against his face.

"Think she'll walk along the canal with him like she did with Major Disaster? We had a good spot there, except for the prickles."

42

"Nearer the bridge would be better. We could see them for longer."

"Hey!" Joe turned, the earring still swinging. "How about if we did it like a relay? One of us could spy outside the pub while the other one goes further along the bank. Then when they come out—'

'—The first one goes to where the second one was, and the second one nips round the bend till they come back."

Holly grinned with satisfaction. It didn't do for little brothers to have the last word. "We'll need two notebooks," she said.

The phone began ringing again.

A low evening sun shimmered on the Wallcot canal, strands of candyfloss cloud drifting above it. No one would guess dead fish lurked below that glittering surface. Joe's class had just finished a project on pollution. He looked at his watch. Seven two and twelve seconds. Say they were going to be in the pub an hour. Better start looking out just before eight. Add on about twenty minutes' spying time plus ten minutes to get home . . . Should be OK. He stretched out in the sunshine and prepared for a long wait. Was it always this warm in April? Here he was thinking swimming trunks wouldn't be a bad idea and the football season wasn't over yet. It'd be murder playing the semi-final in a heatwave, although Piggy Foster puffing away in goal for the Maggies might just tip it for Priory Road. Shame Mum wasn't going to be there.

He thought back to the phone call before they came out. Holly had made a dive for the upstairs phone a good ten seconds before their mother picked up the one in the kitchen, and this time she had spoken to him for herself. Sebastian—

43

the *real* Sebastian—had rung again. They'd have to find a way of seeing him if he was going to be a regular. Shouldn't be too difficult now they knew where Teresa took them. And they'd both heard his voice so between them they'd be sure to recognize it again.

It had sounded quite a nice voice, Joe remembered, surprised at himself for giving away points to one of *them*. Quite deep, and with an accent he didn't recognize. Holly said it was Scottish. But whoever it belonged to, Teresa had cut him short. She'd only been on the phone about thirty seconds, then rushed up to say goodbye looking hot and flustered.

Maybe Sebastian wasn't nice at all. Maybe he'd been pestering her. Men did that sometimes on the phone. Or maybe she'd just been hot from rushing around before she went out. Joe yawned and unwrapped his half-packet of biscuits, then focused the binoculars on a crowd of chattering rooks across the canal.

Holly spat on her hand. It wasn't as easy as it sounded, this spying business. Sliding down the canal bank she had come to a sudden halt behind an extremely prickly hawthorn bush, and her hand had found the middle of a nettle patch. But she had a bird's-eye view of the Rose and Crown beer garden. Trying to ignore the stinging red pinpoints coming up on her fingers she scanned the tables. It seemed to be a more popular pub than the others; it took her a good few minutes of shifting and shuffling before she spotted her mother's new blue top. That was her, in the far corner. But, this time, Teresa didn't look awkward or uncomfortable. She was laughing. Laughing and talking and looking thoroughly relaxed, while the man opposite leant forward and smiled into her eyes.

It was Sebastian. This one had to be Sebastian. The way

he was eyeing her up and down as though he wanted to eat her. Pestering her on the phone, smarming round her, pretending to be Mr Universe. It all fitted. Fighting off a wave of panic, Holly scuffled and slid another six feet down the bank, screwing up her eyes, trying to get a better look at the monster who was about to steal her mother from her. 'Monster' wasn't so far off, either. Stick a pair of tusks on him and he'd pass as something out of the Natural History Museum. She began shooting death-ray looks at the huge figure squashed into a flimsy plastic chair.

Everything about him was hairy. Even his hair was hairier than other people's. It was long and loose and wild, and joined up with the beard below to make a kind of shaggy mane round his face. He wore a hairy, grey jumper with holes in the elbows and a pair of faded jeans. Sticking out beneath them were long, hairy toes that wiggled in open sandals. As he talked he waved hairy hands about and fed himself crisps non-stop through a gap in the mane. Loudmouth, Holly thought. You could have heard his voice the other side of West Merton. But it wasn't, she realized suddenly, the voice she had heard on the phone. It still wasn't Sebastian. She didn't know whether to feel relieved or disappointed.

Making a spyhole in the undergrowth she watched him carefully. The hair, the sandals, the hard, brown look of outdoor living. A hippy? Would they have to live in a broken-down old bus and never go to school? Tragic images of her and Joe barefoot, collecting firewood, passed before her eyes and a terrible anxiety gripped her. Without taking her eyes off the pair of them she demolished every one of her biscuits as Teresa laughed, and the man talked—and talked and talked, until Holly's bottom went numb and she had pins and needles in her legs. Painfully she eased herself into a different

45

position and got out her notebook. "29 April (7.41 p.m.)," she wrote, "The Wooly Mammoth . . ."

As soon as they made moves to leave she scrambled stiffly back up the bank.

"About time!" she muttered, and raced along to where Joe lay dozing in the sunshine.

"Enemy approaching," she panted. "Huge, hairy! Take up new positions immediately!"

Joe leapt awake. His eyes widened as he imagined his mother walking along the towpath with a bear.

"Roger!" he whispered, and sped off round the bend of the canal.

As he watched from the bottom of Donkey Steps he saw what Holly meant. Talk about hairy! And he must be well over six feet tall. She'd get a stiff neck talking to that one for more than a few minutes, and as for *kissing* . . . They crossed the bridge and paused on the other side, then strolled past the moorings. The man seemed to be explaining something about the boats to her. They peered at ropes and woodwork, read the names on the sides, chatted to the people on board.

"Get a move on!" Joe grumbled.

Eventually they disappeared from sight and he scribbled his own notes, then hurried back to Holly.

"What happened? Did they do anything?" she demanded.

But Joe was looking anxiously at his watch.

"It's nearly twenty-five past eight," he said. "Mum'll kill me if she finds out I was late home."

Holly stuffed everything back in the rucksack.

"OK, Plan B," she said. "We'll have to go back through Clegg's."

Clegg's was a small bakery that sat between the canal and Priory Road. Its yard backed on to the school playground. If you fancied yourself as a bit of an athlete and weren't bogged down with shopping or bikes, it was possible to use it as a short cut. In spite of the manager's threats and Mr Wilkinson's warnings, most of the Canal Street children regularly came that way to school. But Exeter Gardens, where Holly and Joe lived, was on the other side of Priory Road, a good ten minutes away. Clegg's was Joe's only hope. He played out strictly on trust when Teresa wasn't around. If she discovered he'd taken advantage she could ground him for a week. It had happened before.

They took Donkey Steps two at a time, then ran panting up Water Lane.

"You first."

Holly shoved him over the wall. A few strands of barbed wire still stretched along the top, but they had been trodden down by so many feet they no longer presented any real challenge. What were a few scratches in the cause of freedom? She hoisted herself up after him and they ran round the buildings and across the yard. Through the side gate, over the fence. She stopped.

"Wait!"

Joe shot her an agonized look.

"It's practically half-past, Holly. I *can't* wait!"

Without turning her eyes she beckoned him urgently back. Joe hesitated then, muttering with impatience, clambered on to the fence again. He peered round her into the school playground, and stared in disbelief.

"Crikey O'Reilly! What's going on?"

Chapter Six

The doors of the old garage stood wide open, the carefully packed and labelled tea chests dragged out and tipped over. A sea of jumble spilt from them. Clothes, toys, books, ornaments lay smashed and scattered across the playground. As Holly and Joe watched, four or five boys waded into the wreckage, kicking and hurling it at each other, howling with laughter. Kevin Foggarty was there and so was Denim Jacket from the park. Joe would have known him anywhere. They trampled on clothes, wrenched toys apart, ripped pages from books. Some of them had scrawled graffiti on the garage doors. Then Denim Jacket got out a box of matches.

"Right, lads." He grinned a wide, stupid grin. "Bonfire Night's arrived a bit early this year!"

He struck a match and held it to the heap.

Holly put a hand to her mouth and Joe saw she was almost crying. If he'd spent half the week sorting out twelve tea chests of jumble, he'd feel like crying too. But why did these things always happen at the worst possible moment? Eight twenty-nine and twelve seconds.

"I've got to get home," he whispered. "We can phone the fire brigade from there."

They slid off the fence and squeezed into Priory Road.

"Pigs!" Holly panted as they ran. "Rotten stinking *pigs*! All

48

that work, all the stuff everyone's brought in. What's going to happen on Saturday now?"

She thought of the hand-drawn posters, the promises of cakes, the rotas of helpers and tea-makers.

"I *hate* them!" she wailed—and ran smack into a man with a dog. All at the same time, the dog leapt up barking, Joe yelled, "Watch out!" and Holly lost her footing. She landed painfully on her bottom, her heart pounding, and found herself confronting two long brown corduroy legs.

"Well now," a voice said. "What's all this?"

She looked up into the familiar face of Mr Wilkinson.

"Oh, sir!" She scrambled to her feet. "Sir, some boys are setting fire to the jumble! They've tipped it all out and now they're going to burn it. You've got to do something, sir!"

Mr Wilkinson stared, first at her then at Joe.

"How do you know?" he demanded. "Have they forced the gate?"

Joe rushed to his sister's aid.

"No, sir, we saw them, sir! Just now from the top of Cle—"

He bit his lip. Holly rolled her eyes at him.

"I see." Mr Wilkinson looked at them intently. "In a hurry to get home, were you?"

"Yes sir," Joe said miserably. "I'm supposed to be in by half-past eight . . ."

He looked hopelessly at his watch. Eight thirty-two and twenty-eight seconds. So much for short cuts.

"Any good with dogs, are you?" Mr Wilkinson asked suddenly. To his surprise Joe felt a leather lead being pushed into his hand.

"Perhaps you'd be kind enough to keep an eye on young Rufus for me. I'll collect him when I've dealt with those jokers—though experience tells me *that* may take some time.

Take him home if you like; he knows how to behave." He leant closer. "You never know, he may even help to calm the Certain Wrath."

He patted a bewildered Rufus hastily on the head then raced off towards school. Not so much as a word about them being in Clegg's. Holly and Joe looked at each other, then at the long, lean creature that whimpered beside them. It had huge liquid eyes and a glossy chestnut coat. Joe put out his hand. The dog sniffed it.

"Good boy," Joe said. "Good boy, Rufus."

A rough pink tongue emerged and licked his fingers. Joe forgot all about being late home and grinned with delight.

"Come on, nature boy, it's still going to be twenty to nine at least before we get back," Holly said.

They set off again for home, Joe with Rufus's lead wound round his wrist. None of it seemed quite such a disaster now. Mum would be sure to understand if he explained how they'd helped save the jumble. Except she'd probably want to know how they'd found out about it, just like Wilkie. Why was life so complicated? They ran down Priory Road and turned into Exeter Gardens. He'd give Rufus some water when they got in, and a couple of biscuits. Although, should you give dogs biscuits? Just one, then. And he'd see if Rufus knew any tricks, how to play dead or shake a paw. Wilkie had put the dog in his care. He couldn't just go to bed and leave him.

At ten-past ten Teresa walked into the living room to find Joe in pyjamas, wrestling with an over-excited chestnut-coloured dog. Holly, still dressed, was bouncing up and down in an armchair shouting encouragement. There were long red hairs all over the carpet, a dish of water was spilt in one corner, bits of broken biscuit crunched underfoot.

50

"What on *earth* is going on?"

At the sound of her voice Joe slid sheepishly from under the dog's legs. Rufus, leaking at both ends with excitement, leapt up to greet her. Barking joyfully, he tried to lick her hands and face. A vase toppled off the coffee table, a smudged pattern of paw prints appeared down her new cream skirt. Holly groaned and slid down in the armchair, hoping to become invisible.

Their mother gripped the dog firmly by the collar and marched it into the kitchen.

"Right," she said in a voice they recognized. "I want to know exactly what's going on and I want to know now! Just what is that dog doing here?"

Joe watched the water from the spilt vase spread in a dark stain and felt a piece of biscuit sharp under his knee.

Mayday, he signalled to Holly. *Mayday!*

"It's, um, Wilkie's dog, Mum. You know, Mr Wilkinson from school." Her voice came out squeaky. "We were just looking after it for him while he sorts out the fire—some boys were vandalizing the jumble, Mum. We saw them! It was all over the playground and they were going to set fire to it, but then we bumped into Wilkie, so we told him, and he asked us to look after the dog. We couldn't say no, could we, Mum? We'll clear up the mess, I promise."

Teresa looked hard at both of them, then asked exactly the same question as Mr Wilkinson.

"If all this was going on in the school playground, how did *you* manage to see it?"

Joe felt the wet patch reach his pyjamas. He stood up. Surrender was the only option.

"We went through Clegg's," he confessed. "But I'd only have been five minutes late if we hadn't met Wilkie, Mum,

51

honest I would. We were going to phone the fire brigade when we got home."

Teresa sighed. She opened the kitchen door and the dog flew straight to Joe.

"Look, Mum, he likes me!" Joe said proudly. "His name's Rufus."

The dog rolled on its back and Joe rubbed its soft pink stomach.

"Can we have a dog, Mum?" he begged. "I'd look after it, I would really."

Teresa surveyed the room, then closed her eyes.

"What I need now is a good strong cup of coffee. And *you*'ve got exactly five minutes to get this lot cleared up."

The kitchen door closed firmly behind her and Rufus rolled hopefully on the floor once more. No takers. He shook a coatful of soggy crumbs across the room then curled up on the rug.

"Oh, no, you don't!"

Holly took his collar and Joe followed them out to the porch. She tied Rufus's lead to a plant stand.

"I won't be long, boy," Joe told him. "Be good now."

The place did look a bit of a mess. Only water and crumbs though, wouldn't take a few minutes to clear up. He set to work with the dustpan and brush while Holly mopped up the water.

"She's mad at us, isn't she?" he whispered.

"What do *you* think?"

"I think I'm probably grounded for a year. Do you think she'll be mad at Wilkie, too?"

Holly shrugged, trying to pick wet dog hairs out of the cloth.

"If she's not," Joe said hopefully, "he might let me take

Rufus for walks sometimes. Now that he knows me . . ."

They put their heads round the kitchen door to report mission completed, then escaped upstairs.

"Conference first," Holly reminded him.

In the excitement of the jumble sabotage and dogsitting, Joe had completely forgotten about Codename Sebastian. If it hadn't been for that stupid man sounding his mouth off half the night he wouldn't have been late back at all. But then he wouldn't have had Rufus to look after, either. A picture of that night's Sebastian rose in his mind. He shuddered. They'd probably have to pick hairs out of the carpet after him, too. He pulled out his notebook and read again what he had written.

"Too tall. Torks too loude. Carnt see his face under hare. Scruffy jumper." Then he had added grudgingly, "Mum likes torking too him." Suddenly he felt tired. He stumbled wearily into Holly's room and sat down on the bed.

"What've you got on him?" he asked.

Holly read out her own notes.

"Resembells prehistoric monster. Long frizzy beard and mustarsh, very unhyjeanic. Shows off. Eats other poeple's crisps." She paused. "Makes Mum laugh."

"What do you reckon for Father Factor?" Joe said. "I gave him three."

Holly raised her eyebrows.

"You never *liked* him?"

"Well, if Mum did . . ."

She chewed her pencil.

"Two and a half."

In spite of their efforts to stay awake, neither of them heard Mr Wilkinson collect Rufus or what their mother said to him.

But in the morning the vase was back on the coffee table, the carpet vacuumed, and the rug showed no trace of dog hairs. Teresa had left for an early shift. A note lay on the table.

Mr Wilkinson says thank you for looking after his dog. Have to see one of my old ladies at five, Mrs Bryant's getting tea. If you play out the deadline's still eighty-thirty. I'll be waiting! Love Mum.

Joe's eyes popped.

"I'm not grounded! Do you think she's all right?"

"If she is, you'll have Wilkie to thank for it," Holly said shrewdly. "I bet he caught them."

Even before assembly the school was buzzing with the news that Mr Wilkinson had surprised a gang of fire-raisers. No one knew how he had discovered them, but Kevin Foggarty wasn't in school, and at playtime Holly and the other jumble sorters were summoned to Wilkie's room. He was wearing his sad bloodhound face. Four glasses of orange juice and a plate of doughnuts sat on his desk.

"You know what I'm going to ask," he said mournfully, "but I'm hoping bribery will do the trick. Have some orange juice, have a doughnut. Have two doughnuts. And how would you like to miss afternoon lessons for the rest of the week?"

"It's all right, sir, it won't take long to get straight again," Holly's friend, Debs, said.

"We weren't going to start pricing till today," Holly added.

"Are we really going to be let off lessons every afternoon?" Ian McEnnis was overcome at the thought. No hymn practice, no extra maths with Mrs Carmichael. Barry Collins gave him

54

a warning nudge. It didn't do to appear too enthusiastic, Wilkie might take some of it back. But their headmaster smiled benignly.

"I knew I could rely on Priory Roaders. You four shall have the very first go on the new computer we're getting out of all this. Here, have the rest of the doughnuts. Take them back for your friends."

"Thanks, sir!"

Ian McEnnis's face lit up. Then he frowned.

"Er, I don't like doughnuts very much, sir."

With one accord Holly kicked him, Debs hissed in his ear and Barry Collins nudged him so hard he yelped.

Chapter Seven

"If I hear 'God Save the Queen' once more I shall scream!" The washing-up water sloshed dangerously near the edge of the sink.

"He's got to practise, Mum." Holly excused the halting squeaks and groans coming from her brother's trumpet. "We're on first, and the junior band's got a spot later."

Mr Wilkinson's latest brainwave had been to add musical entertainment to the jumble sale's list of attractions. She piled the dry dishes in the cupboard and hung up the tea towel. "He sounds all right with the others."

"He'd better," Teresa warned, "or everyone'll be running home with their fingers in their ears before they even see that mountain of cakes I was baking till midnight. I'll bring them in about twelve, but I can't stay. There's shopping to do, this place is like a pigsty, and we're shorthanded with the old ladies again. I said I'd do three till six."

"That's not fair, Mum! You never come to school things now!" Holly looked put out.

"Someone has to earn the bacon." Teresa put an arm round her. "I'll be here all day tomorrow."

"What about tonight?"

"Er, going out."

Her mother moved away and Holly stood against the sink, watching her.

"Mum," she said. "What are they like, the men from this club? Are any of them nice?"

Teresa shrugged.

"Depends what you think's nice. They're all on their best behaviour, but some people's best behaviour isn't up to much, you know!"

"Tell me about them," Holly begged.

Teresa hesitated, then left the basket of washing and pulled a chair up to the table.

"One of them was called Arnold," she said. "A Captain, no less. Captain Arnold Hetherington-Phillips, British Army, retired."

Major Disaster, Holly thought. It had to be Major Disaster.

"Did you like him?"

Teresa leant across the table.

"He told me what to drink, what to wear, what to put in my curries and how to counter-attack against the enemy. He used the most obnoxious aftershave and never stopped talking about himself once. You'd have to be mad or desperate to like someone like that!"

Holly gave a little shudder of relief.

"Haven't there been any you did like? That you liked talking to, at least?" she asked craftily. A smile crossed Teresa's face.

"There was Ozzie," she said. "I hadn't enjoyed myself so much in years."

Ozzie. A tight band of jealousy closed round Holly's chest.

"So he's a possible, is he?" she said carefully. Teresa threw back her head and laughed.

"Not unless you fancy living in a tepee off seaweed sandwiches, spending your weekends looking for King Arthur's grave! What a character, the things he'd done! Made *my* life seem incredibly boring."

57

And although that appeared to be the Woolly Mammoth disposed of too, Holly felt a vague concern.

"You're not boring, Mum," she said. "You're special. Don't any of them want to hear about you? What *you*'ve done, what *you*'re interested in?"

"Bless you." Teresa squeezed her hand. "One or two," she admitted.

"Like—Sebastian?"

"Heavens, is that the time?" Teresa jumped up. "Here we are gossiping the day away with all this work to be done! Enjoy yourselves at the jumble—don't forget your instruments. I'll see you later."

She slipped into her jacket, grabbed a shopping bag and disappeared out of the door. Holly looked after her thoughtfully. Then Joe came through to the kitchen and she realized "God Save the Queen" had ended a while back. He opened the valve on his trumpet and dribbled water on to the floor.

"Looks as though we're safe for a bit," he grinned, and Holly knew he had been listening from the next room.

"Can't you do that somewhere else? Other people don't want to slide about in your disgusting spit!" she snapped. Joe looked at her in surprise.

"It's condensation, not spit," he said. "What's biting you?"

Holly didn't know. But it had something to do with wanting a bit of her mother all to herself.

The noise hit them before they even got through the door. Half of Wallcot seemed to have invaded Priory Road School and the other half seemed to be queuing outside. People were dragging things, dropping things, bumping into things, practising instruments, testing loudspeakers. They threaded their way through the stalls and dumped their belongings in

58

the TV room, then went back into the hall. Holly and Debs were on children's books and Joe was helping with toys. At least he was supposed to be helping. But it was far more tempting to play with the piles of cars and games and little figures than arrange them.

"If you're going to mess about," a sixth-year told him, "you can go and help Mrs Carmichael on teas."

Joe had his bit of stall ready in minutes.

"Is your mum helping?" Debs asked Holly. "Mine's on plants, and my dad's carrying in the furniture."

Such was the power of Mr Wilkinson's persuasion that people had even offered armchairs and bookcases to the jumble sale. Holly could see Debs's dad's strong arm would come in handy. She wondered what it would be like if their own father was still at home, how it would feel to say "Dad" as often as she said "Mum". She couldn't imagine it now. Was that a good thing or a bad thing?

"Mum's working this afternoon," she said, "but she's bringing some cakes in later."

"Chocolate?" Debs asked hopefully.

"Probably."

"Remind me to sneak out and get some before they all go."

How someone as skinny as Debs could be a chocaholic remained one of life's great mysteries.

On the dot of two Holly raised her clarinet to her lips and the school band burst into a ragged fanfare. Parked either side of the entrance hall, they had been entertaining the waiting queue like buskers. Then, after a few words from Mr Wilkinson, the hall doors opened and the crowd surged in. Holly watched them in astonishment. Heads down, charging anyone in their path, they reminded her of one of those cattle stampedes in westerns. She half-expected to hear the thundering of hoofs and see a cloud of dust rise behind them. Squeezing through the crush she made her way back to children's books.

"Keep your eyes peeled and don't turn your back to give change," Debs whispered.

Holly stared as her friend yanked a picture book from under an old lady's coat. A man opposite took a scarf from the clothes stall and simply strolled off, winding it round his neck.

"Do people always pinch things from jumble sales?"

Debs seemed to have a better grasp of these things than she did.

"Always," Debs said. "We have lots at church, it's the same every time."

Could you get arrested for jumble-sale lifting, Holly wondered.

Within minutes, though, she had no more time to wonder about anything. For the next two hours the school hall heaved with a mass of grabbing, snatching, munching, swilling bargain hunters. Holly made a mental note never to work in Woolworths. But by four o'clock the worst was over. Most of the stalls looked as though a crazed burglar had been let loose on them and just a few weary souls still braved Mrs Carmichael's stewed tea. A lot had been sold, though, and Wilkie stood smugly, pouring pop for the helpers. The grownups were meeting in the Butcher's Arms later, Debs's mum had said.

Joe appeared, staggering under three games, a bag of Lego and a collection of cars that looked as though they had come off worst in a motorway pileup.

"I'm going back to Spud's house with the team," he said importantly. "We're discussing Tactics."

"Looks like it!" Holly grinned. "See you teatime. Don't forget we're *on* tonight."

She piled their instruments into Debs's mum's car and went off to check the new rabbit's progress.

But by half-past six the fine spring weather had broken, and it was raining. Not just spitting or drizzling, but real rain falling down in hard bouncing sheets. Mrs Bryant washed up in spite of Holly telling her not to, then paddled off under an outsize umbrella to get her husband's supper. Holly watched her go down the path, then turned away from the window.

"Can't see Mum and the latest Sebastian sitting out in this," she said. "Got any ideas?"

Apart from his "asking for the toilet" routine, which he wouldn't dare do in such a small pub as the Rose and Crown, Joe was equally stumped.

"Looks like we'll have to give up on this one," he said.

Holly bit her nails with frustration.

"But suppose it's *the* one, the one she falls for? Keep thinking. There's got to be a way!"

As they sat, foreheads creased in concentration, the door slammed and Teresa came through shaking her hair.

"What a night!" she exclaimed. "Had your tea? Everything go all right?"

Joe pointed proudly to the bits of Lego and the miniature scrapyard littering the carpet.

"Your cakes went first, Mum," Holly told her. "Wilkie thinks we made loads of money. He gave us all pop and crisps for helping."

Teresa flopped into an armchair and slipped off her shoes. "Any chance of a cup of tea?"

"I'll get it," Holly offered. "Going anywhere nice tonight?"

"Well, I *was* going to give big Ozzie another try, just for the fun of it," she said, "but I chickened out. It'd be cruel to string him along. Anyway, Carol caught me at the jumble and made me promise to look in at the Butcher's Arms."

The children exchanged glances. Good for Debs's mum.

"Just got to pop back and see one of my old ladies first, make sure she's settled for the night. I can do it on the way."

She took the mug of tea, hauled herself from the chair and disappeared upstairs.

"So that's all right then."

Joe settled down to a serious invasion of the scrapyard by a collection of one-armed, one-eyed raiders. "Do you want to play a game later? There's nothing on telly, and it's only got a few bits missing."

"Mmm, later."

Holly was curled up on the sofa with one of her bargain books. "I've just got to an exciting bit."

Teresa came down, her hair freshly washed, changed out of her nurse's uniform.

"Don't need to buy you two anything for Christmas, do I? Just send you out to the nearest jumble sale."

"Mum!" Joe rose to the bait.

"Shan't be late. Just feel I ought to show my face," she said. "There are some left-over jumble cakes in the tin. Help yourselves."

Missiles and fireballs exploded among the wrecks on the carpet as Joe's men fought valiantly to defeat the enemy. Holly chewed her nails as the children in the book fled from the creeping forest fire. So when the telephone shrilled neither of them registered the first few rings. Then Joe emerged with a jolt from battle and Holly abruptly left the Australian bush. She reached the phone one pace behind him and craned her neck to hear who it was.

"Um, she's not here," Joe said.

He twisted his head round, mouthing "Sebastian!" Holly yanked the phone from him in time to hear a deep Scottish voice say, '. . . had hoped to catch her before . . .'

It was *him* again! Why was he still phoning? Why hadn't Teresa packed him off with the rest?

"Mum's gone out," she said firmly. And suddenly inspiration struck.

"You see," she explained in a more confidential tone, "every night she has to go and put our Great Aunt Esmerelda to bed and stay with her till she goes to sleep. Otherwise she gets upset and throws all her bedclothes out of the window. Great Aunt Esmerelda that is, not Mum."

Her imagination blossomed.

"And before that she has to bath the triplets. But tonight Timothy tried to drown Thomas, and Thomas wedged Tilly's big toe up the tap. She didn't stop crying for hours. So—so Mum was very tired after all that and she'll definitely want an early night when she gets back!"

Joe's mouth had gone slack with astonishment. Sebastian coughed down the line.

"I see," he said. "I had no idea your mother possessed such an—er, extended family. Perhaps I'd better leave things until they're a little calmer."

The receiver clicked and Holly looked smug.

"That's got rid of *him*," she said.

Chapter Eight

But it hadn't. He rang three more times during the next two weeks, twice when Teresa was working late and once after she'd just got in. The third time Holly stood on the stairs clutching her toothbrush in alarm as muffled laughter came through the wall.

"Timothy . . ." she heard, then, ". . . Esmerelda!"

Sweat broke out on her forehead. But Teresa said nothing, and Holly began puzzling how they ever made arrangements to meet. They surely hadn't spent all this time making thirty-second phone calls. He could ring her at work, she supposed, but it didn't seem likely. Even she and Joe weren't allowed to do that except in an emergency. And where did they go when they did meet? All those hours watching the Rose and Crown, working out observation points and escape routes, timing the journey home (including the emergency dash through Clegg's). Yet not one of the Sebastians they'd seen had a voice that matched his.

There had been plenty to choose from. As the weather turned fine again Holly and Joe had got to know the canal bank almost as well as their own backyard. The Codename Sebastian dossier swelled as Twitchylips, Egghead, Tarzan and Humpty Dumpty joined Major Disaster and the Woolly Mammoth. But none of them rated more than a miserable two and a half for Father Factor, and none of them managed to persuade Teresa into a second meeting. Only Sebastian remained a regular. And then, at last, the day before the Merton and Wallcot Schools' Cup Final, there was a clue.

Joe was over the moon about Priory Road getting through. They had beaten St Margaret's five–two, with Spud carried from the field shoulder-high. Toasts were drunk, backs slapped, highlights relived. Joe had come home drunk on Coke and glory. For the rest of the week he had talked about nothing else.

"Only one team can win, you know," Teresa warned him Friday teatime. "And Merton County have taken the Cup home three years running."

Joe was scornful.

"They're rubbish. We'll beat 'em hands down!"

"You'd better," Holly giggled, "or you'll be done for fouling!"

"Very funny!" Joe turned to his mother. "How come you know so much about Merton County, Mum? You're not changing sides, are you?"

"Course not," Teresa said quickly, but Holly eyed her mother keenly. For someone who'd never shown any interest in football before she did seem to know an awful lot about it these days. Dates and times of matches. Who'd won what. Which teams were in line for the Cup ... Absently she dribbled salad cream on to her fish fingers. The craziest idea had begun to form in her mind.

"Watch what you're doing!"

Teresa grabbed her wrist. The puddle on her plate was in danger of becoming a swimming pool. Holly pulled her thoughts together and sent a chip in to paddle. Crackpot, she told herself. It had been a pretty wild idea.

65

They finished tea with the sun still pouring into the kitchen.

"I can't remember a May like this for years," Teresa said. "I hope we don't pay for it later."

It was funny how people said that, Joe thought. As though you were only allowed a certain amount of sunshine and after you'd had your share it would rain for the rest of the summer.

"So long as it's fine tomorrow," he said, crossing his fingers.

"Will you be late tonight, Mum?"

Holly couldn't face yet another account of how soundly Priory Road were going to slaughter the opposition. Teresa pushed back her chair.

"Shouldn't think so," she said, "though it's a pity not to make the most of these light evenings. You two playing out?"

Holly nodded.

"We might go down the park."

"Well, remember the deadline's still half-past eight. Champion footballers—and their supporters—need their beauty sleep!"

She disappeared upstairs and Holly and Joe began clearing away the dishes.

"Is it me on the pub tonight, or you?" Joe whispered. Holly worked it out.

"You did Humpty Dumpty, I did Twitchylips and Egghead . . . you tonight. Good, a night off getting stung!"

"You should look where you put your hands," Joe told her smugly. "I've never been stung."

"Only because you try to do it by remote control!"

She knew Joe watched from much higher up the bank than she did because he was scared stiff of Teresa spotting him. He shrugged.

"I can see just as well from up there, and I'm not taking

66

any chances tonight. Nothing's going to spoil tomorrow!"

"Sure you ought to risk walking at all?" Holly's eyebrows rose sarcastically. "I mean, you don't want to wear your legs down overnight, do you?"

Joe gave her a withering look and tripped over the rug.

Teresa went out at six-thirty. Earlier than usual, Holly noted, and her mother seemed to be playing this one very cool. None of the usual comments about how he sounded or what he did for a living. Perhaps because it was a Sebastian she'd seen before ... Holly froze. The only Sebastian she'd definitely seen more than once was the very first one. The *real* Sebastian. Holly did some rapid calculations. How long since the first phone call? Six, seven weeks? Say they'd seen each other once or twice a week since then—though lately Teresa had been disappearing more often. What did that come to ... twelve, fifteen meetings! *Fifteen meetings!* They were practically married, and she and Joe hadn't even managed to get a look at him yet. Codename Sebastian took on a sudden new urgency.

"Binoculars?"

  "Yep."

  "Notebooks, pencils?"

  "Yep."

  "Camera?"

  "Aye, aye, skipper."

  "Biscuits?"

  "Sure thing—coconut and chocolate chip."

Joe repacked the rucksack and slung it on his shoulder. Too warm for jumpers tonight. As Holly closed the front door behind them she squinted into the sun.

"How about going the other way for a change, down Donkey Steps and back along the towpath? Debs said they're getting the barges ready for the boat festival. We could see what's going on."

"OK."

They set off in the direction of school. Funny, Holly thought, in winter they'd be sitting by the fire watching telly at this time, and outside it would be dark and freezing cold. It was lucky Teresa had joined her club in the spring. There was no way they could have gone Sebastian-spotting in January. They turned the corner of Priory Road and Joe sprinted ahead, the rucksack bouncing on his back. At the top of Donkey Steps he turned.

"They're putting flags on the boats, come on!" he called. He ran down the steps and across the bridge to the moorings.

"Only for a little while," Holly warned. "She's changed her routine tonight, we mustn't lose her."

They sat on the bank, watching the activity. Some of the boats were plain dark red or green, but others had pictures of castles and roses and shiny brass fittings. People scurried about with brushes and blow-torches, painting, polishing, rubbing down.

"Want to earn a few bob?" a man called. "Special rates for good workers!"

Joe perked up. Any mention of cash set his antennae quivering, but Holly looked at her watch.

"No chance. Come on, time to move."

She dragged him back across the bridge and they followed the towpath until the Rose and Crown came into view.

"Checkpoint," Joe said, and Holly nodded. She pulled her share of the biscuits from the rucksack.

"You sure we've got the same? Yours is bigger than mine."
She poked the bags suspiciously.

"There's eight in each," Joe told her. "Look, if you don't believe me."

She counted them out on to the grass.

"Satisfied?"

Holly shrugged and picked up her rations. She had stuffed them into her pocket and turned, about to scramble up to the sentry post, when a shadow fell across the path. Two large pairs of black boots crunched to a halt beside her and a horribly familiar voice spoke.

"Well, look who's here. Just in time for supper, too!"

Holly went numb. Even without lifting her eyes she knew exactly who the voice belonged to. Within seconds a dozen different thoughts had skittered through her head. There'd be trouble. Joe would be bullied again. They'd steal the binoculars, the camera. Teresa would find out what they had been doing . . . Willing her hand not to shake, she held out the bag of biscuits.

"Coconut and chocolate chip," she said. "Would you like one?"

Denim Jacket grinned.

"Learnt a few manners, eh?"

He grabbed the bag and peered inside. Then he shook his head.

"Oh dear," he said. "These won't go far. My little brother here's very hungry. We wouldn't want him to starve, would we?"

Kevin Foggarty smirked as the older boy reached forward and twisted Joe's biscuits from his grasp. Tight-lipped, Joe released them. But the pickings had come too easy and the boys hung around.

"Nice day." Kevin sprayed a shower of biscuit crumbs over them.

Denim Jacket nodded at Joe.

"You're looking a bit hot, kid. Need cooling down, I shouldn't wonder."

Kevin laughed.

"Don't suppose he brought his swimming trunks with him. Did you, Burgess?"

Holly looked at him sharply. Surely they couldn't mean . . . ? A cold stone of fear lodged in her stomach. They wouldn't dare! She glanced quickly at Joe, but he didn't seem to have caught the boys' meaning. They lay stretched out on the grass beside her, crunching biscuits, casually exploring the contents of the rucksack. They peered at each other through the binoculars, pretended to take photos, opened the dossier . . . Suddenly Holly couldn't bear it. A burst of panicky anger erupted inside her.

"You've had your fun!" she spat. "Done your stealing and bullying for the night. Why don't you push off and leave us alone!"

Even before she had finished speaking she knew it was a mistake. They turned slowly towards her. The older boy's eyes narrowed. He bent his head so close his breath touched her face.

"We never bully or steal," he said, gripping her shoulder hard. "You better remember that, little girl. But pushing off, now there's an idea . . ."

He got to his feet.

Joe looked up confused as they grabbed his arms. Then, as he found himself being dragged towards the canal, realization dawned.

"Get off! Pack it in! Help! Murder!" he yelled, so loudly

70

the people on the boats turned to see what was happening. One of them called to the boys to stop it.

"We're only messing about. It's a game!" Kevin Foggarty called back.

But it wasn't a game and they all knew it. They forced him nearer the edge, gripping him tighter the more he kicked out. Joe struggled wildly, his shoulders burning in their sockets as he wriggled and twisted. But there were two of them, and they were both bigger than him. Tears and sweat ran down his face. His heart hammered in his ears.

"Holly, help me! Help!" he sobbed.

Holly looked round frantically for a weapon. Something— anything—to stop them. Her eyes lighted on the binoculars. They were the large, old-fashioned kind; long metal eye- pieces, a focusing dial the size of a cake cutter. Without thinking, she grabbed them and twisted the strap round her fist. Then she swung them hard at Denim Jacket. He was a large, stocky boy and it was a thick jacket. If she could just distract him, surprise him into loosening his grip. But at the exact moment they whizzed through the air, Joe's elbow ground backwards into Denim Jacket's stomach and the boy folded in pain. With a sickening crack the binoculars met the back of his head. For a few seconds he crouched over the canal, staring stupidly. Then, without a sound, he toppled slowly into the water.

Chapter Nine

She had killed him, she must have done. Headlines leapt into her mind.

LIFE FOR WALLCOT WATER TORTURER!

TOWPATH TERROR SENT DOWN!

She was a murderer. She'd have to go to prison. Never see Mum again, or Debs, or Joe. She stared, panic-stricken, at the spot where he had fallen in. Then the boy's dark head surfaced like a seal and he made a weak spluttering sound. Holly breathed again. Immediately her brain whirred into action. A stick, they needed a stick to pull him in. She turned and found Kevin Foggarty, frozen with shock.

"Do something useful for a change!" she snapped. "Find something for him to swim to!"

But Kevin stood, ashy faced.

"He can't swim," he muttered.

"Can't swim?"

The two of them had been going to push Joe in, to chuck him in that disgusting water without any idea whether *he* could swim. Without even caring if he drowned. The boy in the water coughed and called and went under again, and Holly automatically pulled off her shoes and socks. All those

72

bricks she'd dived for at the baths, all those medals people flashed around at swimming club. This was what they were really about. She looked into the canal's cloudy depths and shivered. If she hesitated now she'd never do it. For a moment her toes curled white on the edge. Grey water. Dark waves. She closed her eyes and plunged.

"Keep still!" she shouted. "Tread water—I'm coming to get you!"

But the boy had been taken over by terror. As Holly came within reach he grabbed at her, arms and legs threshing in panic.

"Turn over, I'm going to tow you!" she yelled.

But all sense seemed to have left him. He clutched her blindly, retching and spitting, his fingers clamped fast to her T-shirt. If she couldn't free herself he would pull them both under. She looked desperately towards the other bank. Already some people from the boats were stripping off.

"Help!" she yelled. "Someone help me! I can't do it!"

But before any of them could dive in, another figure sliced through the water behind her. Too big for Joe, he headed straight for the terrified boy, then raised an arm and slapped him hard across the face. The boy gulped and swallowed. Holly slipped quickly from his grasp. Gripping the boy firmly round the chest, the man began dragging him to safety.

"It's all right, Holly," he called. "I've got him! Get yourself back now."

Holly struck out for the bank without even wondering how he knew her name.

Dripping and shivering, her teeth chattering, she grabbed Joe's hand and hauled herself on to the path. People were hurrying across the bridge with rugs and towels. Before shock or cold could bite into her she found herself stripped and enveloped in a cocoon of warmth.

"That's better, my love," a woman from the boats said, rubbing her down. "Could have caught your death in there—or something worse!"

Holly looked round for Joe. No chance of keeping this a secret. They'd probably have reporters knocking on the door tomorrow. And they'd need a *very* good story to explain what had been going on . . .

Joe came anxiously towards her—and for a moment Holly's head spun. The canal water must have affected her brain. It was an action replay. She was seeing things. Wasn't that a leather lead in his hand and a large chestnut dog on the end? They'd just come through Clegg's. The jumble was on fire. She'd fallen off the fence and banged her head . . . Then she saw the limp figure of Denim Jacket being hauled from the water and, beside her, a pair of sodden brown corduroy legs.

"Oh, sir," Holly said. "You again!"

Mr Wilkinson peeled off his shirt and shook a shower of drops from his hair.

"Where would you be without me, that's what I'd like to know," he said.

"Sir, they were bullying Joe, they were going to push him in!" Holly tried to explain. "I didn't mean to hit him on the head, really I didn't. I just wanted to stop them . . ."

Shock took her over and she burst into tears. Wilkie crouched beside her, a towel round his neck.

"It's all right, Holly," he said. "I saw it all. He asked for everything he got."

Holly rubbed a hand across her eyes. The people walking along the towpath must have seen, too, she realized, and

74

everyone on the boats. Maybe she wouldn't have to go to prison after all. To her surprise quite a crowd had gathered. She scanned the bank, hoping there was no one there she knew, and suddenly she spotted the rucksack. In the drama of the rescue she had forgotten about it. It lay where the boys had thrown it, the contents still strewn across the grass. Rapidly she counted camera, binoculars, notebooks, even the empty biscuit bags. Then she saw the dossier. It lay wide open at the first page. "CODENAME SEBASTIAN" stared up at her in capital letters.

Frantically she sent out signals to Joe. Put it *away*, she mouthed, get it out of sight. But Joe's mind seemed entirely taken up with Rufus. Holly fumed helplessly, the dossier just beyond her reach. With only a blanket between her and the world she didn't dare move too quickly. She had no desire to appear on page three of Saturday's *Wallcot Gazette*. But as Wilkie turned to talk to someone she stretched out a foot. No good. Too far away. She gathered the blanket round her and shuffled forward on her bottom. Her toe nudged the dossier. Better. She reached out a hand. Another inch . . . a centimetre . . . her fingers closed round it. Thankfully she snapped it shut and pushed it back in the rucksack. She looked up. Wilkie was watching her.

Sweat broke out all over Holly's body. Had he seen? Had he read what it said? But it was only a page with a weird heading, he couldn't possibly know what it meant. Calm down, she ordered herself. Change the subject, take his attention away.

"Will *he* be all right, sir?"

She nodded towards Denim Jacket who was being vigorously massaged by a couple of men from the boats. Kevin Foggarty had mysteriously disappeared.

Wilkie's face darkened.

"Carl Bellingham? Aye, he'll be all right, the girt daft galoot! No thanks to him you didn't both drown in that stinking jaw-hole!"

Holly stared and he gave an embarrassed laugh.

"Sorry." His face changed to the sad bloodhound expression he wore at school. "Blame it on a northern childhood. Long time ago now, but the words still slip out when I'm angry. At least no one down here knows what they mean, though!"

The north. He came from the north. How far north . . . ? For a moment her eyes held his. Then a voice called out that tea was ready and he turned away. Holly struggled to her feet trying to look as though she walked around wearing nothing but a blanket every day of her life.

They all squashed into the tiny cabin and Holly wriggled gratefully into someone's spare shorts and T-shirt, then warmed her hands round a mug of hot tea.

"Feeling better, love?"

The woman with the blanket looked her over critically. Holly nodded, avoiding Wilkie's eye. The sooner they got out of the spotlight the better. The last thing they needed was publicity. As soon as she could, she dragged Joe away from his ecstatic reunion with Rufus.

"Thanks for the clothes," she said. "I'll bring them back tomorrow."

She picked up the plastic bag with her own wet things.

"No hurry, my duck, whenever you're ready." The woman moved to let her pass. "Sure you're all right now?"

Holly nodded. She looked awkwardly at Wilkie.

"Thanks a lot for helping us, sir."

76

They waved from the bridge and set off for home.

"Carl Bellingham," Joe said. "There's a Lee Bellingham in the infants. Do you think it's his brother?"

He had been toying with the idea of terrorizing him at playtime, then decided it wasn't fair. Holly shuddered. "Leave him alone," she advised. "We won't have any more trouble with the big one. What a wimp, can't even swim!"

"Funny Wilkie being there again, wasn't it?" Joe said. The same thought had occurred to Holly.

"Lots of people walk their dogs along the canal," she said, quickening the pace. "Come on. I want to get these things washed before Mum gets back."

"We've got hours yet." Joe looked at his watch. Seven fifty-three and nineteen seconds. "But I think I'll stay in now. I don't want anything else to happen before tomorrow!"

Holly stopped. She had forgotten all about the Cup Final.

"You all right? They didn't pull your shoulder out or anything?"

Joe shook his head. Then he grinned.

"You were brilliant. Spiderwoman Battles with the Beast! Deep in the Amazon jungle Joe Burgess, fearless explorer, was about to be thrown in the crocodile-infested Orinoco—"

"You read too many comics," Holly told him.

They turned into Exeter Gardens and crossed the road. If she put both lots of clothes in the washing machine straight away they'd be done easily before nine. Then they could plan what to tell Teresa. The main thing was why they'd been by the canal when they were supposed to have been at the park. Still, plenty of time to sort that one out. They let themselves in and she dumped the bag of wet clothes in the porch.

"Want some orange?" she called. "Even after all that tea, I've still got the taste of canal water in my mouth."

"OK."

They went through to the sitting room.

"Do you know," Teresa remarked, appearing from behind the kitchen door, "I could have sworn you just said canal water. It'd make a change from Coke, I suppose, but I don't see it catching on myself."

She headed towards the table with a large dish. Then her eye caught the yellow of Holly's borrowed T-shirt and she stopped. She took in the strange shorts, Holly's damp hair clinging to her face. She set the dish down and stared.

"What on earth have you been doing? Whose clothes have you got on?"

"Mum! You—you were going out. You weren't here . . ."

Joe spluttered to a standstill. He looked desperately to his sister for help. But for once Holly was struck dumb. She simply stood, twisting and untwisting the hem of the yellow T-shirt, unable to utter a word.

"Well?" Teresa prompted. "Have you been to a clothes-swopping party? Or perhaps you were mugged by second-hand T-shirt raiders? And I can't wait to hear where canal water comes into it."

She pulled out a chair and sat facing them. Arms folded. Waiting.

Chapter Ten

Twice Holly opened her mouth then closed it again. She reminded Joe of something ... Spud's goldfish. Same expression. He tried willing her brain back into action, but the excuse mechanism had clearly suffered a major breakdown. She stood zombie-like, guilt written all over her face. Joe cleared his throat. Tonight it was going to be up to him.

"Mum," he announced. "Holly just saved my life."

Teresa's eyes widened. He saw shock. Alarm. Then she looked at him hard.

"How—saved your life? What have you been up to? And what were you doing by the canal? You told me you were going to the park."

Joe blinked. He hadn't thought out a story. He looked helplessly at Holly, and at last the cogs began to turn.

"It was the—um—the boats, Mum," she began. "We wanted to see them getting ready for the festival but we thought it—um—might upset you if we said because of going there with Dad and everything. So we just went anyway. But then these boys came along and had a go at Joe, trying to push him in. Only one of *them* fell in instead and he couldn't swim so—"

"—So Holly dived in after him!" Joe took over. "Except he struggled so much he nearly drowned her. But Wilkie got there just in time and—"

"*Wilkie?*" Teresa looked at him intently. "Do you mean Mr Wilkinson? Your headmaster?"

Joe nodded.

"It was dead lucky, Mum. He was walking Rufus again and, Mum, he remembered me! Rufus remembered me! Anyway, Wilkie got this boy out, Carl Bellingham he's called, and then the people from the boats came over with towels and things and made us go back with them. We had to drink loads of yucky tea with sugar in, then a lady lent Holly some clothes and then we came home . . ."

What was it Holly had said about catching smugglers? Seeing if they sweated or blushed? Look innocent, he told himself. He tried a sickly smile. Holly wiped wet palms down the back of her borrowed shorts. It wasn't telling lies exactly. Just twisting the truth round a bit.

Teresa let out a sigh, half-relief, half-exasperation.

"What am I going to do with you two? You need a nanny—or a policeman! At least you're both safe, that's the main thing." She felt Holly's forehead. "No shivers, no sneezes? Sure?"

Holly shook her head.

"I'm fine, Mum, honest." Her mother looked at her.

"Did you really try to save that boy? You actually dived into the canal after him?"

Holly nodded.

"I don't know that *I* would have done. Probably wouldn't have had the guts."

Holly reddened and Joe's eyebrows rose.

"But you should never have been down by the canal in the first place," Teresa went on. "Heaven only knows what's been dumped in that water. You're going to Dr Parsons first thing in the morning for a checkover. And it's out of bounds from now on. Understood?"

"Understood."

They exchanged looks. So much for Sebastian-spotting. There was a point where imaginative thinking became straight lying, and Holly didn't think she was prepared to go that far. It would be too complicated, anyway. The excuses, the stories, the risk of being found out. They'd have to find some other way of carrying on the detective work.

"What happened to the boyfriend tonight, Mum?" she said. "Didn't you like him?"

Teresa busied herself at the draining board.

"He, er, didn't turn up. Not to worry. I expect he'll be in touch."

Holly watched her carefully. She was acting pretty cool for someone who'd just been stood up. And there was something else odd. She had just heard that Joe had been bullied and Holly had nearly drowned. They were her children, for goodness sake! You'd think she'd be a bit more worried. Keep looking at them, asking if they were all right, that sort of thing. But she hadn't even checked Joe wasn't hurt. She almost seemed happier now than when they had first come in. Fishy, Holly thought. Very fishy. Her mother turned to Joe. "An early night for you, young man. You've got a big day tomorrow."

"I wish *you* were coming, Mum."

Teresa ruffled his hair.

"We're already three nurses down," she said, "but I'll try and get there for the second half. OK?"

Holly's frown deepened. All this stuff about being short of nurses, but usually she was able to change shifts whenever she wanted. She hadn't seen the semi-final either, and even at the jumble sale she had just whisked in and out. It was almost as though she was avoiding school things, yet she'd made cakes for the jumble and still took her turn washing the school strip. And she always knew exactly what was going on. Holly picked up the rucksack and slipped out of the room. She had some serious thinking to do.

Up in her bedroom she propped the Codename Sebastian dossier in front of her. None of it had come to much, but at least they'd got a look at the opposition. She ran her eye down the list.

1. MAJOR DISASTER
borring bighead, loud voice
2. BIG OZZIE a.k.a. THE WOOLY MAMMOTH
possible, not likely
3. TWITCHYLIPS
about 100 years old, no hair
4. EGGHEAD
said University 17 times
5. TARZAN
musceles, tattooes
6. HUMPTY DUMPTY
fat, round, laugh like a highena

That just left Sebastian. The real Sebastian. But they knew no more about *him* than the first day he had phoned. Or did they . . . ? Think detective, Holly told herself. Turning to a new page she wrote CLUES. Then she drew a line down the middle and chewed her pencil. At ten to ten she sat back, her heart fluttering, and looked at what she had written.

MUM
1. Is'nt interested in football but knew about Merton County and when the semy final was. HOW?

2. Did'nt ground Joe when he was late back and Roofers messed up the house. WHY?
3. Does'nt come to school things any more. WHY NOT? (still helps)
4. Did'nt get in a state about the canal buisness. WHY NOT?

SEBASTIAN
1. Talks with Scottish acksent. IS IT REAL?
2. Knows when Mum's in. DOES HE PHONE HER AT WORK?
3. Dose'nt go to Rose and Crown like other Sebastians. WHY NOT?
4. Could have something to do with football. WHAT?

But she had stopped short of spelling out the wild, woolly-brained idea that had moved into her head and wouldn't go away. Instead, against every clue she had written simply JSW. She read through the list again then pushed the dossier safely into a drawer. There were a couple more things to check before they could be sure. But then they'd know. They'd really know.

MERTON COUNTY MURDERED!!
By Special Corispondents Joe Burgess and Emma (Spud) Clarke

At 9.30am on Saturday Priory Road (with a practickerly unbeaten home record!!) came out in thier posh new green and yellow strip and made a FANTASTIC! start against cup holders Merton County. After only four minutes pacy striker Clarke lammed in thier first gaol and six minutes later thier second one was helped in

83

the net by a Merton deffender (thanks boys!!) there was a narsty moment when the Blues Bradshaw should have scored but as ushual it just sored over the crossbar although Carkhill sneeked the ball in the net ten minutes from halftime. But Priory Road's Secret Weppon in the number 9 shirt SPUD CLARKE!! foght back and slamed in gaol number three as the whisle went.

HALFTIME SCORE: PRIORY ROAD 3
MERTON COUNTY 1

Merton County's torcher continude in the second half allthough a penalty by Bradshaw acturly went in!! and somehow the ball sliped passed a fantastic fingertip save by Priory Roads ace keeper Williams. But a centre from the prommising Burgess let Simms smash in Priory Roads FOURTH! gaol!! and the Blues defenses were riped apart. After that Priory Road killed them with hot shot Spud Clarke the best striker THEY HAVE EVER HAD!! clinching the game with gaol number five two minutes from time. Merton County fought gallently but they couldnt match the Priory Roaders style.

FINAL SCORE: PRIORY ROAD 5   MERTON COUNTY 3

Joe put his pencil down on the final draft. Not only had they won the cup, but he and Spud had been given half Monday morning off lessons to write up the game for the school newsletter. It had to go to Wilkie for final approval, then Mrs Brady in the office would print it out. By Friday everyone would have a copy.

"Terrific game!" Joe said for the hundred and seventy-third time. Spud nodded.

"Terrific!"

They laid the sheet of paper on Mr Wilkinson's desk, then went off to join the dinner queue.

Holly had been looking out for him. She elbowed her way through the starving hordes and grabbed him by the collar.

"Wait for me after school," she hissed. "We've got to check something."

"About Sebastian?"

She nodded.

"Tell you about it later. Meet me outside Julie's. Don't forget!"

She disappeared into the crowd. Julie's was the sweetshop round the corner from school, and Joe found one part of his brain already calculating whether he had enough for a packet of something. But another part of it was racing feverishly because he, too, had been doing some hard thinking. And then, just before dinner ... A wave of half-scary, half-delicious possibility washed through him when he remembered what he had seen.

Promptly at three-forty Holly extracted him from the 2p display in Julie's. She was in one of her businesslike moods.

"Where we going?" Joe asked, running to keep up.

"Library," she said shortly.

"Why?"

"Register of Electors. Miss Marshall told us about it. Everyone who can vote is on it. It tells you their *names*," she added significantly.

"But who are we looking up?" Joe asked, though he thought he already knew. Holly stopped and pulled the Codename Sebastian dossier from her bag. She gave it to him open.

"Read that," she said.

Joe saw the heading CLUES and the two columns underneath. Agonizingly slowly he read through them. Then he went through them both again. Holly waited, biting her lip.

"Well?" she demanded, and Joe frowned.

"How d'you know about JSW?"

"School notepaper. It's at the top of every sheet. Head Teacher J.S. Wilkinson, B.Sc. M.Ed."

"I saw it on his briefcase," Joe said.

Now it was out, it seemed both more real and more impossible than it had inside their heads. The clues certainly added up. But to an answer that carried all the worries and problems that real things always did. In a way it had been easier having lots of Sebastians to worry about. Less scary than one particular one . . . The picture that had haunted her for two days rose sharply in her mind, and she snapped the lid shut on her thoughts.

"Better check," she said.

They pushed open the door of the library and climbed the stairs to the reference room.

"It's for a project," Holly told the librarian. She was handed a thick, heavy book.

"It's all in streets, not names," Joe whispered. "And we don't know where he lives."

He stared shiftily round the room at a few silent browsers. He had never been in this part of the library before. Holly leafed through the register, not knowing where to start.

"It's probably somewhere quite posh, but it's got to be close to the canal if he was walking Rufus there."

"He might have gone in the car."

She ignored him and flicked through the pages till she came to Wallcot ward.

"Why does it say 'ward'?" Joe said. "I thought that was in hospital."

"It means the area." Holly's class did Junior Citizenship. "So everyone doesn't have to vote at the same place."

They skimmed through lists of streets, not getting anywhere.

Joe recalled his carol-singing route.

"What about Grosvenor Crescent? That's posh." Holly made a face.

"Too posh, they all have Range Rovers down there."

They checked Grosvenor Crescent twice all the same. No Wilkinsons.

"Let's try Lapwing Lane," she suggested next. "That's got big houses but they're kind of crumbly, not really rich. And they've got long gardens. For Rufus."

She thumbed through the register until she found the right page. Odd and even numbers were in separate columns, and it was a much longer road than she had thought. But near the end of the evens, on number ninety-two, her finger stopped. There it was. Wilkinson, Jack S. To their disappointment there was absolutely nothing to show what the "S" stood for. It might as well have been Samson or Shakespeare as Sebastian. But worse, much worse, there was another name below his.

Wilkinson, Angela C.

The images Holly had been pushing down since Saturday rose vividly in her mind. The woman at the Cup Final who had left before Teresa got there . . . The little girl who slipped from her arms . . . "Dad!" she had called to Wilkie.

87

"Daddy!" He had turned away from Holly's stare, embarrassed. Or ashamed. Her face drained of colour. Joe shook her, puzzled.

"What's the matter?"

But Holly hardly heard him. There was a buzzing and a ringing in her ears, a cackling of cruel laughter. Pictures tumbled about in her mind. Dad and Karen. Mr Foggarty and Mrs Roper. Wilkie climbing out of the canal, Wilkie pouring pop at the jumble sale. Laughing, cracking jokes, playing the fool . . . but all the time he'd been conning them. He'd conned them all. He was a cheat. A liar. Lying to them, lying to Teresa. Holly was filled with a terrible sadness.

"He's married," she said.

Chapter Eleven

She laid the register heavily on the counter and Joe followed her downstairs, his mouth tight and dry. But as soon as they were outside he turned on her.

"You don't know that!" he stormed. "You don't even know it's Wilkie! There could be *hundreds* of Mr Wilkinsons in Wallcot! Just because he's got the same initials doesn't mean it's him."

"I saw her," Holly said. "At the Cup Final. And there was a little girl."

Joe was silent. All he had been aware of was the game.

"I don't believe it," he said at last, obstinately. "Wilkie wouldn't do that." But a tiny flicker of doubt crossed his mind all the same. You only had to look at the paper or the telly to see that an awful lot of grownups did just that most of the time.

"Well, I'm finding out," he announced.

Rummaging in his pockets he pulled out two headless figures, a polythene-bag parachute, half a packet of crisps and an elderly chew coated in grey fluff. He wished now he hadn't spent all his spare cash in Julie's.

"Got any 10ps?" he said.

"You're never going to ring up and ask!"

Joe looked at his sister patiently.

"You're not the only one with a brain, you know.

Look, there's two things we want to know about Wilkie. Whether he's Sebastian and whether he's married or not. Right?"

Holly nodded.

"So first we check it's his house, then I say the football team wants to get him a present. That's not a lie, it's going to be one of those tankard things with his name on. Spud thought of that. So then I ask her what the 'S' stands for so we can get it right."

"But if *she* answers we'll know he's married."

"He doesn't have to be. It could be his—his mother."

Holly remembered the long silky hair, the smile that passed between them.

"Not old enough."

But Joe's face had set. He picked up the coins and marched off to the phone box.

Crammed into the tiny space, Holly's heart beat wildly as they got the number from directory enquiries. She felt unreal. The whole thing felt unreal. It was like when you stepped off the helter-skelter and your head carried on spinning. Like looking down from a high window. But suppose there really was an explanation. Suppose Joe was right. She hadn't realized how much she wanted him to be.

". . . Sorry to bother you," Joe was saying. "I'm phoning for the football team . . . Priory Road, that's right. Um, the thing is we want to get Wilkie—Mr Wilkinson, I mean—a present. It's going to be a tankard with his name on but we didn't know . . . Oh right, thanks." He widened his eyes dramatically at Holly. "What? Um, we haven't got all the money in yet but . . . Right, I will. OK, then, thanks very much, *Mrs Wilkinson*. Pardon? Oh, we thought . . . But the little girl . . . Oh, sorry . . . Thanks. Goodbye."

Holly knew before he put the phone down. Before he had even got the words out.

"It's his sister!"

Joe's face looked as though it could split with grinning.

"I told you! I told you, didn't I? I knew he wouldn't con anyone!"

"All right, all right, brainbox." Holly felt strangely mean. "We had to check, though, didn't we?"

"*I* didn't," Joe said. "Only about his name. And guess what? His middle one's S-E-B—"

Holly punched him.

"Get on with it! Tell me what she said."

"I'm telling you, aren't I? First she said the bit about being his sister. Then she said she's on a course in East Merton, so she's living at Wilkie's. She helps look after the little girl because her mum died when she was a baby. Good touch calling her *Mrs* Wilkinson, eh?"

He smirked. It wasn't often he got one over on Holly.

"So what's her name?"

"Angela," he said. "You saw it in the register."

"Not the sister, dumbo. The little girl."

Joe thought.

"Rebecca, I think she said."

Rebecca. A little sister. Joe read her thoughts.

"You don't even know if they're getting married yet!"

Something began fizzing and popping inside Holly's head, shooting out crazy little bubbles of excitement.

"Bet you they do!"

She punched him again, happily this time. Then she slung her bag on her back and raced home.

*

91

"What on earth has got into you two?"

Teresa sat at the table, exasperated by all the meaningful looks and giggles.

"Whatever it is, I hope it's not a fixture," she said. "I've got some friends coming on Saturday—I don't want them thinking I live with a couple of turnip heads."

"Friends?" Holly was instantly alert. "What friends, Mum? Who are they?"

But it was Teresa's turn to be mysterious.

"Oh, just a couple of friends from my club. Haven't had anyone round for ages. I thought it was time I showed off my cooking again."

A *couple* of friends. Holly's mind churned out horrific combinations. Major Disaster and Egghead. The Woolly Mammoth and Humpty Dumpty. Twitchylips and Tarzan . . . But, surely Wilkie—Sebastian—was going to be one of them? Although, if he was as special as they thought he was, why was she inviting someone else as well? They must have got it wrong. Wilkie wasn't Sebastian. Sebastian wasn't even special. A whole forkful of chips slid down her throat and lodged painfully at the bottom.

"Why two of them, Mum?"

Her voice came out as a croak. Teresa shrugged.

"They get on pretty well together. No reason why they shouldn't both come," she said.

Joe choked on a sprout. She'd been seeing someone else, she must have been. *Two* someone elses, in fact. And they'd missed them. But how could they? All those hours of spying and checking and writing reports. Unless she'd been meeting them in the daytime. The creases in Holly's forehead told him she was as puzzled as he was. Think football, he told himself. Tactics. Try a different approach.

He put on an upgraded version of the sickly smile.

"Are we invited too, Mum?"

Teresa looked at him shrewdly.

"I thought I'd leave you two a couple of crusts in the outhouse."

He laughed politely.

"Only if we knew who was coming," he persisted, "we could think of interesting things to talk to them about. You know, be more polite. Like the queen. You want us to have good manners, don't you?"

His mother kept her face straight.

"How wonderful to have brought up such civilized children," she said. "When you put it like that I can hardly refuse."

Joe sneaked a victory glance at his sister.

"So if you *really* want to impress, you'd better start reading up on caledoniology, osteology . . . and arboriculture."

She began clearing plates away.

"Cally *what?*" Joe turned to his sister as the kitchen door swung to. "Do you know what she's on about?"

Holly shook her head warningly as Teresa reappeared with the pudding.

"Later," she whispered.

And for the rest of the meal, even while they washed up afterwards, Joe couldn't get another word out of her. How could it be Wilkie coming, he puzzled, if there were going to be two of them. It could be Wilkie and someone else, but why would she invite someone else? She hadn't even *liked* any of the other Sebastians except the Woolly Mammoth. And she'd already shown him the red card.

Would he even want Wilkie to come to their house, Joe suddenly wondered. It was weird when you thought about it. The man who took your school assemblies and told you off for forgetting your football kit being your mum's boyfriend. But if they got married . . . His heart thudded in a way he had come to know well over the past few weeks, only this time he forced himself to think what it would mean. Draw two columns, his mind said in Mrs Carmichael's voice. Bad things first.

Number one: someone else bossing him around. Joe hesitated. Usually Wilkie got you to do things without you feeling you *were* being bossed around. All right, number two: people at school sending him up. But he wasn't sure about that, either. Most people thought Wilkie was great, they might even be jealous. So what else? The house? Yes. Someone else taking up room in the house. He might even have to share a room with Holly! Although . . . it wasn't a very big house, and it certainly wasn't at the posh end of town. Wilkie probably wouldn't want to live there.

But at the thought of moving from Exeter Gardens, a sudden fierce loyalty rose in Joe towards every gutter, fence and gatepost of it. Number twenty-eight, especially the cluttered shoebox of a room that was his, seemed all at once the most desirable place on earth. So how was it, then, that in another part of his mind a sneaky kind of greed was creeping in for a bigger room, a bigger house? A Lapwing Lane kind of house, with a long garden for a dog . . .

"Here, Rufus!" he heard himself call. "Good boy, Rufus! Shan't be long, Mum, just taking Rufus for a walk . . ."

Holly was looking at him oddly.

"Are you going to stand there talking to a tea-towel all night? Those words Mum said—I think I know what one of them means."

Joe flicked the tea-towel at her, embarrassed at being caught daydreaming.

"I can't even remember what they were! How are we supposed to look them up if we can't even spell them?"

But when they were safely upstairs in Holly's room with the door shut, it wasn't a dictionary she started thumbing through but an old school book.

"Last term's English book," she explained. She flicked through it until she came to a page headed "Handwriting". "This is it. Miss Marshall never makes us do it, but when she was off ill once we had crabface Carmichael. We had to copy out this boring poem for hours without talking."

"Same with us," Joe said. "Every Tuesday morning."

He peered at Holly's almost unrecognizable best handwriting.

> O Caledonia! Stern and wild,
> Meet nurse for a poetic child!
> Land of brown heath and shaggy wood,
> Land of the mountain and the flood . . .

"That second word," she said. "Caledonia. I'm sure it's like one of the words Mum said, only there was a bit more to it. Caledon . . . something or other."

"Ology?" Joe offered. "What's it mean?"

"Looks like something to do with a country."

She opened the big dictionary from downstairs. "B . . . C . . . Ca . . . Can't see any caledoniology. Oh, wait a minute . . . Wow, look at this!"

She shoved it under Joe's nose and he read it for himself. "Caledonian. (Native) of ancient Scotland . . ."

Well, Wilkie must be pretty old.

"So—is it him after all?"

But there were going to be *two* visitors. Perhaps he was

95

bringing his sister, or the little girl. Holly was equally puzzled.

"If we could remember the other words they might give us a clue," she said. "Think!"

Joe frowned.

"Didn't one have 'osty' in it? And the other one was like 'agriculture', except it wasn't that exactly, just like it."

"Let's have a go at 'osty' then." Holly turned to the "O"s.

But the only word that began like that was "Ostyak", someone from Siberia. None of the Sebastians were Siberian, as far as she knew. Anyway, it didn't have "ology" on the end. But as her eyes wandered around the place where it should have been, she noticed something.

"Oste(o)" it said on the opposite page. Then, lower down, "Osteology, a branch of anatomy that deals with bones."

"That's it," she said. "It had an 'e' not a 'y'. But Wilkie's not interested in bones, is he?"

Joe shrugged.

"It might be the other person. Have you remembered the third word yet?"

Holly struggled for recall.

"'Arb'—'arber' something . . ."

"'Culture,'" Joe prompted. "Go on, look it up."

She flicked back through the pages, but this time there were no clues at all. It went straight from "arbalest" to "arbiter" with nothing in between.

"Think!" she commanded again. "How else could you spell it?"

She skimmed impatiently down the columns of words. Then, suddenly, as Joe turned the next page, it jumped into view. "Arboriculture, cultivation of trees."

Trees. Bones and trees. Who was interested in bones and trees? Out of the blue the answer hit her.

"Twits!" She smacked her head. "Complete and utter twits, that's what we are!"

Joe was still puzzled.

"What are you on about? Who is it?"

Holly kept her face straight.

"Who do you know who's interested in bones and trees? Very interested, you might say."

She began crawling round the carpet, scrabbling with her hands. Then she lifted a leg against the wardrobe door.

"Woof!" she barked. "Woof, woof!"

For a moment Joe's face registered a blank. Then a kind of diffused raspberry escaped from under the hand he clapped to his mouth. He rolled on the floor, laughing like a drain.

Chapter Twelve

Suddenly Holly couldn't face food. Burgers lay abandoned, crisps tasted like cardboard, even the sight of a sausage made her heave. Every night she heard St James's clock strike twelve, and when sleep did eventually come it brought cackling hyenas and woolly mammoths careering through Exeter Gardens. She woke sweating, then dragged herself to school and slumped at her desk all day, thick-headed and prickly-eyed. She forgot her games kit, her clarinet, her history project. Music practice was abandoned, work left unfinished as she fretted over the possibility of a Burgess/Wilkinson merger. If they *had* to have a stepfather, Wilkie was in a different league from the others. No question. But the thought of what it would do to their lives twisted her insides into knots. New house, new street. New sister. What if they didn't like her? What if she didn't like them? What if Mum liked her *better* than them? Then there was everyone at school. And Dad.

At the thought of her father a hard ball of pain lodged in Holly's chest. Why should they care what Dad said? He hadn't asked their opinion when he married Karen. Face it, she told herself, he's your ex-dad now, he's divorced you. He's not interested any more. She chewed her non-existent nails then started on her pencil. A shade of guilt crept in. In a way he *was* still interested. He sent Teresa money

98

for them, and they always got presents from him on birthdays and at Christmas. But it all seemed to happen at a distance, like sending *Blue Peter* parcels to Africa. She and Joe weren't part of his life any more. She remembered Joe phoning the night his bike was stolen. Dad had never rung back.

Did all parents forget about their first children when they got married again? Holly tried to imagine Teresa promising "I do". The kiss, the ring, confetti, flowers. There'd be a party with a cake and champagne—she might even be a bridesmaid. But all that was just for one day. After the fuss died down they'd be stuck with a stepfather for ever. At least until they were grown up.

It still didn't feel fair having someone dumped on them, even if it was going to be Wilkie. But then it wasn't fair on Teresa, either, sitting at home lonely, while Dad enjoyed a whole new family. Probably you couldn't be fair to everyone at the same time. Maybe Teresa was right, it was time for a change. Time for a new dad. One who'd take them out, go on bike rides, picnics . . . But the thought of calling Mr Wilkinson "Dad" swamped her in a sudden sweaty wave of embarrassment. She ran downstairs and out to the balding patch of grass they called the garden.

Joe was collecting beetles for science.

"Ssh," he warned, "or they'll think you're an earthquake."

"Charming! How many've you got?"

"Three, but there's a shiny blue one here somewhere that doesn't want to get caught."

"Poor thing! How would you like it if you were minding your own little beetle business, and some giant came along and shoved *you* in a jar?"

"It's only for a day," Joe pointed out. "And it's a very

comfortable jar. There's leaves and grass and things, and he won't get rained on. Solar heating, too."

He twisted his piece of stick so that the beetle finally ran up it.

"Gotcher! OK, Mr Beetle, you're on holiday now. Nothing to do but enjoy the scenery and eat the delicious food provided by our first-class chef!"

He fixed a pierced metal lid on the jar and looked at Holly.

"Why've you got shopping bags under your eyes?"

When she didn't answer he picked a blade of grass and tried blowing at it through his fingers.

"Is it because of Saturday?"

Holly nodded. It was all very well having brave ideas about starting a whole new life, but first you had to let go of the old one. Her old one wasn't special, but it was comfortable, familiar. Like old clothes. And it was all she had.

"Suppose they do get married," she said. "Do you realize it would change our whole lives? We'd have to move, for starters, Wilkie'd never want to live here. And Mum probably wouldn't do nights any more. But I like her doing shifts, it gives us more freedom. Then there's everyone at school . . . And I don't even know what we're supposed to call him!"

Her voice wobbled, and a quiver of alarm went through Joe. It wasn't like Holly to lose control.

"We might move to a nicer house," he said encouragingly. He pictured a long garden and a chestnut-coloured dog racing down it. "You might like it better. Mum'll sort everything else out."

Holly scuffed her toe on the path. There was more, he could tell.

"What about Dad?" she muttered. Joe's face closed.

"It's got nothing to do with Dad. Not any more."

But even as he spoke, his mind conjured up a giant cinema screen. Dad swaggering up to Wilkie, thumbs on holsters, spurs jangling. A sneer on his lean brown face.

"No yellow-bellied, weak-kneed Wilkinson bum gets *my* kid . . ." Fat chance.

"And you know Wilkie," he said, trying again. "He'll let us call him anything we want so long as it's not rude!"

But Holly didn't laugh as he had intended. Instead her eyes brightened and blinked, then spilled over.

"Don't—don't you want them to get married?"

A note of anxiety crept into Joe's voice. Holly tore grass from the ground beside her.

"Course I do," she said. "We're going to end up with one of the Sebastians whether we like it or not, and he's about five million times better than the others. It was just—just thinking about Dad. How he doesn't even belong to us any more. Here we are going to get a new stepfather, and even if Dad knew, he wouldn't care. He'd probably just be glad *he* didn't have to bother with us any more!" The tears spilled over again.

"But he *should* care!" She kicked a hole with her heel. "We were his children first. It's not fair!"

Joe's golden vision of the future began to crumble. The disappointments of the past few years slid back into his mind with a horrible ease. All those times he'd phoned and dropped in on his father. All those times he and Karen had been expecting someone, or were just going out, or were busy decorating. He remembered the glances between them, the baby crying, Karen looking at her watch . . . But then a new feeling began to take over. Dad had gone. He had walked out of their lives, and he wasn't coming back. It was stupid to think he would. And now there was the chance of a new

101

dad. One who would probably make a better job of it than their real one.

"We never rated Wilkie for Father Factor," he said. "I think I'd give him ten."

Holly scrubbed at her eyes.

"What we'd give *Dad* is more to the point."

By Friday Teresa had cleaned the house from top to bottom. She bought herself a new dress, mended Joe's favourite jeans and got Holly some new trainers. Not the ones she had been angling for but still, Holly had to admit, pretty good.

"I thought we'd have Chicken Maryland tomorrow," Teresa said. "What do you think?"

"Brill!"

Joe hadn't the faintest idea what Chicken Maryland was, let alone where Maryland might be, but the mere mention of food activated a direct line between his stomach and his brain. Heaven, for Joe, was a kind of long, continuous mealtime with angels hovering in attendance like waiters.

"What's for afters?"

"Lemon cheesecake or trifle, I haven't decided yet."

"Oh, make it cheesecake, Mum! He—I mean *we* like that better . . ."

Holly kicked him and he looked offended. Wilkie often had his dinner on their table at school. He couldn't help knowing he liked lemon cheesecake, could he? But Holly was feeling strong again. She'd managed some shepherd's pie at school yesterday and, to her surprise, the thought of lemon cheesecake was almost pleasant. Whatever had been bugging her must be on its way out.

"We've only got four best plates, Mum," she said. "What's the other one going to eat off?"

102

"The other one?"

"I thought you said you had *two* friends coming." Holly looked innocent. "That makes five. It'll be a bit tight round the table."

Joe swallowed a snort at the thought of Rufus gobbling chicken from one of Teresa's best plates.

"Someone'll have to eat off the floor," he said. His mother looked at him strangely.

"Do you think she knows we know?" he whispered when they were alone. Holly looked up from the bits of paper littering her desk.

"She will if you keep dropping bricks like bombs! *He* likes lemon cheesecake. *Someone*'ll have to eat off the floor."

Joe grinned. "At least it's only Wilkie coming. Imagine if it had been Major Disaster!"

Holly put down the scissors.

"AttenSHUN!" she barked. "Stand by your beds for morning inspecSHUN! Quilts shaken seventy-two times, pyjamas exactly ten centimetres from edge of pillow! Stand up straight. Chests out, stomachs in, show teeth. Aha!" She leered into Joe's face. "An unbrushed molar and a blob of custard on the chin! Forced march to West Merton!"

Joe giggled helplessly.

"Do Egghead now, go on," he begged.

Holly stood up and peered over an imaginary pair of spectacles.

"Oh yerss, my canine is *extremely* intelligent," she drawled. "Teaches osty—thingyology at the UNIVERSITY, you know. I was only saying to Professor Oblotsky the other day—that's Professor Oblotsky from the UNIVERSITY of course—he's a little terror for Chicken Maryland. Sits up a

103

the table scoffing it—but only orff the best plates, of course . . ."

Joe lay on the floor, hiccuping with laughter. Holly covered her desk quickly as they heard Teresa's step on the stairs.

"What on earth is going on up there?" she called. "You're supposed to be getting ready for bed not auditioning for a pantomime!"

"We are, Mum!" Holly called back. "Just got to clean our teeth!" She hoisted Joe from the floor and shoved something under his nose. "Sign it, quick," she ordered.

Joe examined the card carefully. In each corner was a pair of milk-bottle-top wedding bells. Along the bottom sprawled a row of figure-of-eight black cats. The centrepiece was a pair of shiny scarlet cut-out hearts pierced by a hefty dart.

"Who shot that?" he said. "Robin Hood?"

But there was nothing wrong with the lettering.

"Congratulations" it said in neat black felt-tip. And inside, after some undercover research in Julie's, Holly had written "With best wishes for your forthcoming marriage".

Seeing it in black and white like that, Joe had a pang of superstitious anxiety. Something to do with counting your chickens.

"What if they don't get married after all?" he said. "We'll look a right pair of wallies."

"We don't give it to them till we know for sure. But they will," Holly said. "I know they will."

She felt better now, more confident. Something to do with having a pizza and three satsumas inside her. She slid the card into her scrapbook and they padded into the bathroom.

"Tomorrow," she thought as she squeezed, scrubbed and spat. "Tomorrow we'll know for sure."

104

A whirligig of blue froth swirled wildly round the plughole, then disappeared.

"Please, God," Joe prayed. "Please let them get married— and I'll be good for ever. Amen."

Chapter Thirteen

There ought to have been flashing lights in the sky, Holly thought. Angels singing, spaceships in formation spelling out "TONIGHT'S THE NIGHT". But she woke up to a Saturday like any other. In the morning she and Joe went to swimming club, squandered their pocket money in Julie's, then ambled up to the railings above Donkey Steps. Small clouds drifted overhead. A boat hooted on the canal. Everything was normal, and yet . . . Leaning her elbows on the rail, she imagined going home to two parents instead of one. Wilkie's coat in the porch. Rufus curled up on the rug. Beside her Joe swayed gently upside down, arms trailing, watching coloured canal boats glide through a watery sky.

"Do you think she'll say before he comes?" he said.

Holly lay on her arms, eyes closed.

"She'll have to say something or, for all she knows, we might die of shock when he walks in."

"You're *sure* they're going to get married?"

Joe hoisted himself upright, plagued by last-minute fears.

Holly fished out a squashed sherbet fountain.

"Look at it this way," she said. "It's June now and she's been seeing him since April. He's the only Sebastian she's ever seen more than once, and he's *definitely* the only one to

106

get an invite home. So when she practically redecorates the house and turns herself into Miss World in a week, it's got to be serious."

The familiar thudding started up in Joe's chest. Why should he feel so nervous when he *wanted* them to get married? Because he did want it, he really did . . .

The afternoon felt peculiar, unreal. Time seemed to hang, just waiting for the evening to happen. Teresa rushed between bathroom and kitchen, wooden spoon in her hand, her hair a kaleidoscope of coloured rollers. Holly and Joe drifted, unable to settle to anything. Joe fixed something on his bike, ate some biscuits, went for a ride, then slumped in front of the TV, not seeing any of it. Holly read, admired her new trainers, rang Debs. But eventually she trailed upstairs and pulled out the Codename Sebastian dossier. Mud and chocolate spattered its orange cover, and the pages had curled with damp. Battlescarred. It had seen action. She flicked through the pages, going over the clues again carefully, trying to pretend she had never seen them before. Was she just reading into them what she wanted to see, or did they add up? Did they really add up?

Doubts began to sneak in. They had no proof, no real evidence. All they had was a middle name and Wilkie letting slip he came from the north. It might have been Huddersfield for all they knew. There was all that stuff about bones and trees but that could be Mum's idea of a joke—and other people had dogs, too. Suppose they'd jumped to conclusions, put two and two together and made five? Suppose it wasn't Wilkie coming at all? Because if it wasn't him, it had to be someone else . . .

The names in the dossier suddenly stopped being jokes.

107

Major Disaster, Egghead, The Woolly Mammoth. They were real men. Teresa had met them, talked to them, perhaps even done what she and Joe had done and graded them according to a kind of Husband Factor. Holly's insides began churning. It was all very well them sitting there like smug chimpanzees saying "It must be" and "Who else could it be." It wasn't enough. She had to know *definitely*, and she had to know now. She couldn't wait till teatime. She couldn't wait another five minutes. If she didn't find out instantly, that second, she'd go crazy.

The kitchen was full of steam. Saucepans Holly had never seen before sat bubbling on the stove, and a pale moon of cheesecake cooled on the windowsill. The best plates were stacked on the draining board, a clean tablecloth lay over a chair. From the corner of her eye she spotted a dish of water in a corner of the floor. Her pulse quickened.

"Pangs of hunger already?" Teresa glanced up from stirring something. "Help yourself to shortbread—you can give me a hand if you like."

Holly didn't move. She took a deep breath.

"Please, Mum," she said. "I've got to know who's coming."

Holly saw the joke stop on her mother's lips as she turned, saw Teresa take in her skimpy T-shirt, her gangly arms, the gap between jeans and trainers. She wasn't a little girl any more to be teased and played with, to be put off with "wait and see", to be shut out of all the worry and excitement and responsibility of being an adult. She was growing up.

"Please, Mum," Holly said again. "I've *got* to."

Teresa put down the spoon and switched off the gas.

"Yes," she said. "I can see that."

Joe hovered, confused, in the doorway. What was she on

about? They knew who was coming. It was Wilkie, it had to be Wilkie—unless Holly knew something he didn't. Panic washed through him like ice.

"Something tells me it's not going to come as any great surprise," Teresa said. Then she smiled, and Joe felt his heart explode inside his chest.

"It's Wilkie! We know it's Wilkie! It *is* Wilkie, isn't it, Mum?"

He threw his arms round her neck, swinging like a monkey. Teresa put out a hand to steady herself, but for all her laughing she didn't answer. There was a look on her face Holly had never seen there before. She struggled to identify it. Scared. Mum was scared. The thought knocked her back like a blow. Scared of Wilkie? No, stupid, a voice whispered in her head. Scared of saying. In case it doesn't work out. In case it goes wrong again . . .

"We know he's Sebastian," Joe was saying. "Sebastian with the Scottish accent who's always phoning you. We know it's Wilkie's middle name!"

The moment passed. Teresa was back in control.

"So who needs CID with Joe Burgess around?"

"It was Holly, too."

Holly picked at the flaking paint on the back of a chair. Why couldn't he keep his big mouth shut? He'd be bringing out the dossier next. She felt her mother's eyes on her.

"*You*'d want to know," she muttered. "If *your* mum went out with a different boyfriend every night, you'd want to know which one you were getting landed with!"

Teresa laughed out loud.

"Sit down," she ordered. "Sit down, both of you."

She reached across and took their hands.

"Did you really think I'd go out and get you a new dad

just like that? Off the peg, out of a catalogue. Without eve
caring what you thought of him?"

They were silent.

"You two are the most important people in my life," she
said. "There's no way I'd get involved with anyone you didn't
hit it off with—*anyone at all*—so just remember that. I should
have seen you were worrying," she went on. "Phone calls,
strange voices, disappearing night after night. It was just so
good to be meeting new faces, feeling part of the world again.
I never thought of it from your point of view."

And they hadn't thought of it from hers, Holly saw. They
hadn't been pleased she was getting out and enjoying herself.
All she and Joe had cared about was themselves.

"And I'm still worrying about us," she thought guiltily,
"because she hasn't said it's him yet, not definitely . . ."

Teresa squeezed her hand.

"I should never have made such a mystery of it, kept you
in the dark all this time."

Say it, Holly pleaded silently. Just *say* it before I go stark
raving barmy. But Teresa seemed to be having as much diffi-
culty saying it as Holly had asking.

"Look in the corner," her mother said. "It's not a
footbath!"

Holly's eyes returned cautiously to the dish of water. But
Joe let out a whoop.

"It's for Rufus! It *is* Wilkie coming! Go on, Mum, tell us!
Say it!"

Teresa held him away from her, half-laughing, half-
embarrassed.

"OK, OK—I submit!" She let him go and met Holly's
eyes. "You're quite right," she said. "It's him."

Holly's head felt suddenly detached from her body. She

110

gripped the edge of the table. It was true, it really was true. But it was only a meal, it didn't mean . . . As her mind skipped to the hundred dollar question, Joe said it for her.

"Are you going to marry him?"

Holly held her breath. Teresa twisted the wedding ring she still wore. But she didn't say no.

"We both have other people to consider," she said. "I have you two, and he has a little girl."

"Rebecca!"

Joe punched the air and Teresa made a hopeless gesture.

'Ever thought of working for MI5?"

"When do *we* get to see her?" he demanded.

After nine years of being a mere second in command, the thought of becoming an instant big brother was appealing.

"Let's see how things go," his mother said cautiously. "We thought perhaps tomorrow afternoon."

It was the "we" that did it. Jealousy sliced through Holly like a knife. Teresa knew this little girl. She'd talked to her, played with her, held her on her lap. All without so much as a word to them. And now she and Wilkie were already starting to plan things on their behalf. They'd always made decisions together before. Talked, argued, thrashed things out. Was this how it was going to be in future? Her and Joe shut out, kept in the dark? Didn't they count any more? In the warm kitchen Holly felt suddenly alone. An orphan.

"I meant what I said." Teresa held her eye. "There'll be no decisions till we're all sure. But I promise you this. No matter who else comes into our lives you two will *always* be number one with me."

She slipped an arm round Holly's shoulders.

"Come and tell me if the new dress is OK. In the shop I

111

thought I looked like a film star, now I'm not sure which one. Minnie Mouse or Miss Piggy!"

She slid a saucer across to Joe.

"And how about an expert opinion on the cheesecake? We can have fruit salad if it's awful."

Joe poked the mixture suspiciously.

"It's not yellow. You sure you got the right packet?"

"This one's not out of a packet," his mother said. "It's all my own work."

Cheesecake without a packet? Joe had no idea the possibility existed.

"Mum," Holly said, as she helped Teresa squeeze and hook herself into the new dress, "why did you stop coming to school things? Was it because of Wilkie being there?"

Teresa looked guilty.

"I know it was mean, but if I'd had to speak to him—seen him even—I could never have pretended he was just your head teacher."

"But if you liked him so much, why did you go out with all the others?" Holly frowned. "Did he know?"

Teresa smoothed down the dress and looked at herself critically in the mirror.

"I had to be sure," she said. "I hadn't met anyone for so long and Jack—Wilkie—and I got on so well I thought maybe they'd all be like that." She laughed. "They weren't!"

"Didn't he mind?"

"He understood."

Yes, Holly thought, he would. He never made you feel stupid or that you'd got things all wrong. He'd make a nice dad, a good dad . . . so what was wrong? Why wasn't she over the moon like Joe? Because, she told herself, this wasn't just about them getting a dad. It was about Teresa getting a husband.

Joe lingered over the last mouthful of cheesecake. Since Codename Sebastian he had become hooked on Factors. He had invented Teacher Factor, Football Factor, Telly Factor. Now there was Cheesecake Factor. Eight and a half, he decided. It tasted delish—just looked a bit poorly. He dropped the saucer in the sink, then, remembering Rufus's last visit, went into the living room and moved the vase from the coffee table. Sideboard, mantelpiece? He settled on the empty fireplace. It'd be safe there. He checked the water in Rufus's dish and put a couple of digestives on the dresser.

"Cor, Mum!" His eyes widened at the sight of Teresa in her finery. "You look smashing!" Then two little creases appeared between his eyes.

"Um, you're not always going to look like that now, are you . . . ?"

"So much for Miss Piggy," Teresa sighed, and the doorbell rang.

In the ten seconds it took her mother to open it, Holly's stomach qualified for a gold medal in gymnastics. Her heart banged so hard it echoed in her ears. Through a haze she saw Teresa reappear under an avalanche of flowers, Wilkie behind her. He was grinning from ear to ear.

"Hi, sir! Hi, Rufus!" Joe called. A chestnut-coloured whirlwind burst through the door and bounded towards him.

"Down, boy, sit down—you've got to be good tonight!"

To his surprise Rufus sat, his flag of a tail waving furiously as he spotted the biscuits on the dresser. Joe weakened.

"Well, just one then . . ."

He squatted on the rug and held out a digestive.

Tongue quivering, coat flying, Rufus leapt towards him. Too late Joe saw the vase topple, heard it crash. A dark stain began spreading slowly from the fireplace. Holly rolled her eyes. Teresa opened her mouth then closed it again. Wilkie put down the bottle he was carrying, took off his jacket and rolled up his sleeves.

"If you think that one's trouble," he said, "wait till you meet the daughter!"

Chapter Fourteen

From her bedroom window Holly watched the leaves fall. Showers of scarlet, orange, brown. Right at the bottom of the garden, where Lapwing Lane backed on to the park, two gnarled apple trees crouched under an October sky. Joe scrambled up one then leapt across to the other.

"Me now!" Rebecca called.

Holly grinned as he hauled her across. He had got more than he bargained for in Rebecca. Their new little sister reminded her of one of those tornadoes that swept through the USA. Hurricane Rebecca. Four years old, a face full of freckles, and the fieriest red hair they had ever seen. Joe only called her Copperknob once. The right hook that landed in his chest was world class. Served him right. Poor little kid. It must be awful standing out like that, everyone calling her names. Still, better than looking like a cross between a turnip and a coconut.

She turned away from the window and peered gloomily in the mirror. Ears too big, face too pale, mouth full of metal, sticky-out hair. She pulled a face and the turnip-coconut pulled one back. She wasn't really Holly Burgess. She'd been dumped on the doorstep by an extra-terrestrial, and now her earth disguise was wearing off she was changing back into an alien being ... It wasn't just the horrendous brace and the new hairstyle that were different. She'd changed inside as well as out. She wasn't the same person she had been three months ago. All that *worrying*. The Sebastians, moving house, changing schools . . . And now here she was with a high-school uniform, a new sister, and the stepfather they had once been so determined not to have. Jack. For all her worrying he had never asked them to call him Dad, and neither she nor Joe had suggested it. Jack was better. More grown up. Anyway, they still had a dad. Even if he did only crawl out of the woodwork when he smelt something interesting.

The week before the wedding they had an invitation to his flat. Holly could still feel shockwaves run through her, remembering his voice on the phone. In all the time since he had left he hadn't rung once. He said he was sorry for not getting in touch, but things were easier now the baby was walking. He'd got a better job. He missed them. He wanted to see them again. Karen was looking forward to making them a special tea. Karen was *what*? Holly was astonished, then suspicious. How come for four years he had hardly re-membered they existed, then the week before Teresa got married again he was suddenly interested in how they were, where they'd been for their holidays, whether they needed new clothes?

They went, though. Scrubbed and smart, carrying a bunch of flowers. Like visiting someone in hospital. The same polite conversation and long silences. How was school, swimming club, band. Chocolate cake or cookies? Did Teresa still work shifts. Tea or Coke? And then, eventually, what they were really there for. What's he like, what's his house like, well-off is he . . . ? All that was missing was the flashlight in their eyes. Joe was furious.

"Who does he think he is?" he hissed. "Nosing round after all this time, trying to find out our business!"

But Holly had watched her father's fingers twitch nervously on one cigarette after another, Karen's sharp eyes taking in his every move. Perhaps he really didn't want to lose them. She listened to his voice promising things they had once longed for.

"We'll go on the canal . . . For bike rides . . . I'll come to the school concert . . ."

Perhaps he cared after all. But then why had he left them? She pushed away the sharp edge of something that felt like pity. Neither she nor Joe answered.

She crumpled the piece of paper and tried again.

Dear Dad . . . But how did you tell your father you weren't the person he had known? That the tie between you, once so strong and loving, had shrivelled like old elastic? She took out his letter and read it again. She knew it by heart now. Karen was taking the baby to her mother's while he fixed up the kitchen in their new house, and would they like to stay a few days. He'd hire a boat, they could go to Stanney Creek, sleep in it overnight. Holly chewed her nails. She and Joe hadn't been the only uncomfortable ones at the tea party. Karen had looked pinched and pale and hardly said a word. The baby's crying seemed to get on Dad's nerves and he hadn't picked him up once. He kept going on about "old times". The holiday in Cornwall, teaching them to swim. Things they'd done when they were little.

Perhaps it wasn't working out with Karen, either, and now Teresa was off-limits he wanted them back instead. But you couldn't treat people like that. Picking them up and dropping

117

them like toys. It wasn't fair. On the other hand, it wasn't fair for them to dump him, even if he had more or less dumped them. You couldn't divorce your parents, Holly saw, in spite of what she had thought earlier. A little bit of them *was* Dad, would always be Dad. They owed him something. But not spending halfterm playing Happy Families. She and Joe agonized for days.

"It's your decision," Teresa told them.

But she behaved as if it was already made. She went on and on about how much they used to enjoy canal holidays. How they would only mope round the house if they stayed home. How glad they should be their father was taking an interest again. Was that all it was, Holly wondered, or did she actually want them out the way. She could have Jack to herself then. Jack and Rebecca. For a moment Holly pictured herself steering the boat, Dad's hand on hers, Joe fishing off the side. Sunshine, sandwiches, laughing. Like it used to be. She wavered. Not if it was bribery. A way to get rid of them. She picked up her pen again.

"Dear Dad, thanks for the letter. I'm glad the baby's better, perhaps it was his teeth. I'm sorry—" She hesitated, then pressed more firmly. *"I'm sorry but we won't be coming to stay over halfterm. There's lots to do sorting the house out still, and I've promised to take Rebecca swimming. Perhaps,"* she added rashly, *"we could just come for tea one day instead. I hope the new kitchen looks nice. Best wishes from Holly and Joe."*

It was fair, she told herself. Fairer than he'd been. They were people, she and Joe. Not pets or toys. They had minds of their own. And now they were starting a new life of their own. *"PS,"* she wrote. *"We've got a ginger kitten and a rabbit with black ears."*

118

She felt suddenly hollow inside. Empty. Piggy in the middle.

The door burst open and Joe flopped on to her bed.

"Done it?"

"Just about."

"What'd you say?"

"What we decided."

No need to mention about going for tea, unless Dad did. She licked the envelope. The taste of glue lingered on her tongue.

"I thought he sounded a bit—well, sorry about everything now."

She watched her brother carefully, testing the water. Joe shrugged.

"He's only sorry because they've had a row," he said. "Soon as they make it up he'll forget all about us again."

He could be right. Unless . . . unless they had been what the row was about in the first place. Holly slid the letter slowly into her pocket.

"Hang on, I'll get Rufus." Joe stuck his head back round the door. "You seen outside? Mum's digging up worms!"

Teresa squatted on the lawn, a paper sack of bulbs beside her.

"Off out?"

"Only to the post," Holly said. "Um—can I have Debs to stay over halfterm, Mum?"

"Halfterm?" Teresa pierced a hole in the ground, her mind on daffodils. "On the boat, do you mean? With your dad?"

Holly stared down the garden.

"We're not going."

"Not going?" Teresa looked up blankly. "But I thought it

119

was settled. Three days. You're going fishing, taking your bikes. You decided."

"No," Holly said. "*You* decided. *We* want to stay here."

"But—"

Holly watched her suspiciously.

"It's our home, too, isn't it? Why can't we stay here?"

Joe appeared with Rufus. He stopped when he saw their faces.

"I should have thought you'd be glad to see your father again. Goodness knows, you've gone on about him enough!" Teresa pulled off her gardening gloves and threw them down. "It'd be a holiday, a break. We all need one of those from time to time."

Holly stared. She *did* want to get rid of them. She wanted them to go away so she could be on her own with Jack . . . and Rebecca. Joe moved closer and Holly took his hand. He seemed suddenly very small.

"Don't you love us any more, Mum?" she said.

"For heaven's sake!"

Teresa scooped up the bag of bulbs and banged soil off the trowel. "Three days, that's all I'm asking! It doesn't make me into the wicked queen because I want a bit of time to myself. This is not *Babes in the Wood*, you know!"

She's got her fairy-tales mixed up, Holly thought maliciously.

"What about Rebecca?" she said. "She'll still be here. Or doesn't she get in the way?"

Exasperation mounted in her mother's face.

"Rebecca's going to Jack's sister for the weekend. You two were going to your father. And we were planning a quiet few days. On our own."

She picked up her gloves and crammed them into the paper

120

sack. It split, and a cascade of shiny brown bulbs poured out. They rolled crazily through the flower border, under shrubs, into the pond. Joyfully, Rufus began chasing them, trampling them into the damp grass, crunching them, spitting out the bits. Teresa threw down the trowel. It bounced back on to her foot. Very clearly and very loudly she said an extremely rude word.

"Mum!"

Joe's eyes were on stalks. Tightfaced, Teresa limped back to the house.

Holly bit her lip. She pulled the letter from her pocket and looked at it. What were they supposed to say now? *"Dear Dad, it doesn't matter that you took no notice of us for the last four years. Mum says we've got to come and stay. It's her turn to get rid of us now."*

"You two will always be number one with me . . ."

Teresa's voice echoed in her ears, but already they were second best. Nobody cared about them, they might as well be orphans. Viciously she tore the letter across and shoved it in the dustbin.

Teresa was standing at the kitchen window. She looked upset.

"I didn't mean to yell at you. I'm sorry, I really thought it was settled," she said. "But Jack and I didn't have a honeymoon. We've been looking forward to these few days all term."

Holly ran her thumb along the crack in the wall.

"Where you going?"

"Nowhere special." Teresa waved her hands vaguely. "But if you're not going to your dad's . . ."

Holly felt the screws tightening.

"I didn't say we were *definitely* not going," she muttered.

121

Teresa gave her the ghost of a smile and went out to salvage bulbs.

"What!" Joe was outraged. "Course we're not going. We decided! Why do they want to go away without us, anyhow?"

Holly thought back to the wedding. Teresa sewing her bridesmaid's dress into the night. Teresa packing the freezer with sandwiches and sausage rolls. Teresa washing curtains, making up beds, moving mountains of washing up. Boxes, tea chests. Sorting, wrapping, washing. They still weren't properly straight.

"Honeymoon!" Her mother had laughed when someone asked. "This is my honeymoon!"

She had been standing in apron and rubber gloves, knee-deep in old newspapers. Holly shrugged.

"It's kind of a late honeymoon, I suppose. You don't take kids with you on honeymoon."

Only Jack, she thought. Jack and Teresa. Teresa and Jack.

Perhaps they *should* go to Dad's. It might be fun on the boat. He'd be more relaxed on his own, without Karen. And there'd be treats. Bound to be treats . . . She pulled out a drawer and began rummaging.

"What you looking for?" Joe peered in beside her.

"Writing paper. It's only for a few days," she said quickly, seeing his expression. "He'll be different now. I know he will."

Joe's eyebrows met in a single dark line.

"How—different?"

"Because we've got another dad now. He knows he'll have to be careful if he still wants to see us. We don't need him like we used to, not now we've got Jack."

"We haven't got Jack. We haven't even got Mum any more." Joe's lip wobbled dangerously.

"Don't be stupid! Who wallpapered your bedroom? Who bought you dinosaurs for your birthday cake? They just want a couple of days on their own, that's all. It'd be dead boring, anyway. Some old place in the middle of nowhere."

Joe kicked methodically at the cupboard door.

"So—are we going or what?"

"You might like it. We could take Rufus."

He showed a flicker of interest. Holly lifted out the writing pad and something fell to the floor.

A plastic wallet. Papers stuffed in it. British Airways . . . ? She opened it. Plane tickets. French money. She scrabbled in the drawer again. Two little reddish-purple books. Mrs Teresa Margaret Burgess (now Wilkinson), Mr Jack Sebastian Wilkinson. Passports.

"They're going to Paris! It's all arranged!"

Joe grabbed the wallet. He examined the tickets, the foreign money, the passports. Then he examined them all again, as though he hadn't believed it the first time. He stared out at the garden. Teresa collecting bulbs, Jack whistling his way towards the border, spade in hand. As though it was the most normal thing in the world to dump your kids and go off on a foreign holiday without them. Joe threw the wallet on the table. Then very loudly and very deliberately he said *that* word. Holly stared in shocked admiration.

"Mum said it!" Joe was defiant.

Well, anything *he* could do . . . She tried it for herself. Louder. Suddenly they were both giggling.

"What a nerve, getting it all set up without even telling us! Think we'll get a postcard?"

123

"Yeah—Staying in quiet little town, nothing much to do. Wish you were here!"

They pushed everything back in the drawer and Holly took the pad over to the kitchen table. Rufus skidded through the door yelping, bulb skins dangling from his mouth. Joe put an arm round the dog's neck.

"He can sleep in my cabin. Dad won't mind. It'll be his holiday, too." He poked in the bottom of the cupboard.

"We're going to need dog food, biscuits . . ." He broke off to wrestle with Rufus.

"Hey!" He lay back on the floor, a silly grin spreading across his face. "What do French dogs do up lamp posts!"

Holly narrowed her eyes.

"You've just made that up. I bet it's something disgusting." She was dying to know.

"You're dying to know, aren't you?"

Joe rolled over the floor in a fit of giggles.

"Get on with it!" Her foot came dangerously close to his ear.

"All right, all right, I'm telling you, aren't I?" He sat up and grinned idiotically. "Go on, have a guess. Vot does zee French dog do up zee lamp post?" he said in a silly French accent. He didn't often get one over on Holly. She put down the pen and stood up.

"Do you want thumping?"

"*Oui, oui*!"

Bellylaughing, he collapsed back on the floor, arms clutched across his stomach. Holly's fist hovered above his nose.

"No, don't! That's it – that's the answer! *Oui, oui*. Wee wee. Get it? What French dogs do up lamp posts!"

Holly rolled her eyes heavenwards as Rufus leapt promptly on top of him. And did one.

124

PS

Dear Mum and Jack,

We are having a good time ecxept Dad burned the sausiges and everywhere ponged. Rufus likes the boat. He barkes at the other boats. Karen met μs yesterday with the baby. She's not too bad. The baby is cute. Geuss what, we made Dad stop smokeing! Hope youre having a great time in Paris. Can't wait to see you again. We have boght Rebecca a mony box with rabits on.

lots and lots of love from Joe and Holly

xxxxxxxx

Dear Holly and Joe,

Paris is very lively and noisy. The cars toot their horns all the time. We have seen the Eiffel Tower and Jack tried eating snails. He says he'd rather have dog food! The hotel is very posh, unlike our French. Hope you're all enjoying the boat and haven't fallen in. Looking forward to hearing all your news. Love you lots.

Hugs and kisses,
Mum and Jack xxx

PPS

Dear Dad,

Thanks for a great holiday. Mum and Jack had a good time in Paris. They brought us all back Eyeful Tower tee shirts. Rebecca dose'nt like hers. She wanted a monky instead! She can swim a length now (she's only four!!) Jack has finished decerating my room and he has started on Joes. Joe wants it red like Liverpool!! Is your kitchen done yet? I expect we'll see it when we come for tea. We think once a fortnight is a good idea. Don't start smokeing again will you! See you soon.

best wishes from Holly and Joe